# Bond Book ✓

# Falcon and the Carousel of Time

# Falcon and the Carousel of Time

### BY LULI GRAY

HOUGHTON MIFFLIN COMPANY
BOSTON 2005

www.houghtonmifflinbooks.com

The text of this book is set in Dante.

*Library of Congress Cataloging-in-Publication Data*

Gray, Luli.
Falcon and the carousel of time / by Luli Gray.
p. cm.
Summary: When Falcon, her great-great-aunt Emily, and new friend Allie
take an emergency trip to 1903, Blinda Cholmondely
and other old friends try to help them return to the present.

ISBN 0-618-44895-0
[1. Time travel—Fiction. 2. Great-aunts—Fiction. 3. Witches—Fiction.
4. Magic—Fiction. 5. New York (N.Y.)—Fiction.] I. Title.
PZ7.G7794Fah 2005
[Fic]—dc22
2004009211

ISBN-13: 978-0-618-44895-1

Interior design by Pamela Consolazio

Manufactured in the United States of America
WOZ 10 9 8 7 6 5 4 3 2 1

For my sisters: Lizzy, Esther, Doris
and
for my brothers: Don, Dickie, Joe

"Do not go gentle into that good night,
Rage, rage against the dying of the light."

—Dylan Thomas

# CHAPTER ONE

"T O DANCE WITH DRAGONS." FALCON STUDIED THE medal in her hand. A red dragon danced on a cross of gold over the Latin words, *Saltare cum Draconis*. Saint George himself had given it to her last year. The memory flooded her mind, so that for a moment she saw the beach by the Arafura Sea on the north coast of Australia. Her father had looked so small, standing there with the dragon flaming above him against a darkening sky.

She remembered how tiny that same dragon had been when she first hatched out of her hot scarlet egg. Egg had brought Magic into Falcon's life: a saint, a witch, another dragon, adventures through time and space. But magic carries danger as well as delight, and those who find it are forever set apart from ordinary people. And that can be very lonely.

The voice of Dirus, that most fierce and ancient dragon, rumbled in her head: "Girl extraordinary." Falcon's fist closed on the medal, its pin pricking her palm.

"No!" she said, waking Henry, who was sleeping beside her with a paw over his nose. He stretched, arching his furry back. *"Mrrp?"* he said.

"I'm not!" said Falcon. "I'm an *ordinary* girl. I'm normal; I'm just me." Henry curled up again and Falcon reached for the treasure box that stood open on the bed. Her father had brought the wooden chest from Africa, and it held all her most precious things: a shark's tooth from New Zealand; a bowl carved out of a coconut from Brazil; a string of jade prayer beads from Tibet; a silver ring; the ragged remains of a sable hat; and a large piece of scarlet eggshell. Falcon set the medal on top, closed the lid, and put the box in the back of her closet, behind her ice skates.

"It's time for Junior Swim," said Toody. Her kid brother stood in the doorway, wearing swim trunks and flip-flops and carrying a gym bag. He still had a little boy's tummy, but he was beginning to look more like his father, and his face had lost some of its baby chubbiness.

"You shouldn't bite your nails, it could get affected," said Toody. "How come you're hiding your box?"

"I'm not hiding it, I'm putting it away," said Falcon. "You can't go to Swim in just your bathing suit."

"I know," said Toody, pulling shorts and a T-shirt from his bag. A tattered snakeskin protruded from its depths.

"Why do you still have that disgusting old skin? It stinks," said Falcon.

"It doesn't. Egg gave it back to me, she said, 'Rich gifts are pure when givers prove so kind.'"

Falcon scowled at her brother.

"I don't want to talk about Egg, all that . . . that magic stuff anymore. It's too weird and dorky."

"It is NOT!" cried Toody, his face flushed with indignation. "It's, it's . . . splendred!" He stomped out, flip-flops slapping against the floor.

Falcon pulled off her pajamas and grabbed her favorite bathing suit from the closet doorknob. Mei Chu sold Speedos to her students at a big discount, so Falcon had half a dozen suits in her dresser drawer, and she needed all of them. Swimming nearly every day is hard on bathing suits, even if you always remember to rinse out the chlorine after class. Falcon sometimes forgot. She had just started taking Waterobics, which was mostly for grownups; thirteen was the minimum age. Mei's niece Lily Weng was in the class, along with Lily's best friend, Penny Alden.

Lily had been Falcon's best friend till sixth grade, but just before she found the scarlet egg in Central Park, Falcon began to realize that she and Lily weren't interested in the same things anymore. Whenever she suggested they go to a museum on a rainy Saturday, Lily would say, "That is soooo lame. I know! Let's go to Alura and try on the perfumes." She'd meant to tell Lily about the egg and the dragon that had hatched out of it, but somehow she'd never found the right moment. Soon she got so involved with taking care of Egg that she and Lily spent less and less time together; now they never saw each other outside of school. *It's Egg who ruined it,* Falcon thought. *Egg and all that magic.* Now Lily was one of the popular kids at

Chapman, and Falcon was on the outside with no one to talk to except nerds like David Keppler, Allie Cadwallader-Newton, and Maruna Abaz.

One of the good things about going to Waterobics instead of Junior Swim was that it might allow her to be friends with Lily again, which would make her one of the cool kids. Lily and Penny were totally cool.

The other good thing was that she was not responsible for Toody once they got to the pool. He had become a good swimmer. Water was the only thing he'd ever been afraid of, and now that he could swim, he seemed to fear nothing. He had sailed through kindergarten and first grade, oblivious to teasing, holding his own against bullies by turning their taunts into jokes. He just assumed that everyone was his friend and that the world was a fascinating, welcoming place.

Falcon decided to wear the old green suit one last time, and then she'd switch to the yellow and black. She pulled on the suit, covered it with a knee-length T-shirt, and stepped into a pair of sandals. She stuffed shorts, a towel, and underpants into her gym bag and hurried out to the living room, where Toody and Missy were sitting on the couch, holding a copy of *Time* magazine between them and drawing crossed eyes, stuck-out tongues, and buck teeth on all the celebrities and politicians with black markers. Missy's face was flushed from laughing, and for a moment Falcon wished she could join them. The googly face game used to be one of her favorites. She and Missy never played googly face now, or dress up, or marching band either. *It's baby stuff,* she thought. *I'm too old for games.*

"We're late," she said. "Let's go."

4

"I've been ready," said Toody. "I was ready for thirteen minutes."

"Come straight home, babies; don't forget we're having dinner at Ardene's," said Missy, closing the magazine and putting the markers in her jeans pocket. Falcon made a mental note to check pockets before she did the laundry.

Falcon and Toody were supposed to hold hands on the way to the pool, but they had worked out a deal. They held hands just until they were out of sight of the doorman, and Toody had to wait for Falcon at the corners.

"Ardene's making pudding cake," said Toody, "and chicken pot, chicken pot, chicken pot pie." He let go of Falcon's hand and galloped ahead to 78th Street, pulling up with a jerk of the invisible reins he was holding and a loud screech of imaginary brakes.

"Horses don't have brakes," said Falcon, coming up beside him. Toody looked both ways, slapped himself on the right hip, and trotted across the street. "Mine does," he said.

At the Sportsplex on West 74th Street they separated. Toody went to the regular pool, where Mei Chu taught Junior Swim, and Falcon went to the lap pool for Waterobics with Frank, Mei's partner. In the fall she would start Intermediate Swim with Mei Chu, and she was taking Waterobics to fill in till then. It was just aerobics in water, but it was way more fun than exercising on land. A boom box played music to go with the workout, and there was neat equipment like hand paddles and weights. Falcon's favorite was the Aquajogger belt that let you float upright so you could run in the water without putting your feet on the bottom of the pool. No matter how hard you ran, you never actually got anywhere, and for some reason that always made her laugh.

People were already in the water, jogging in place to warm up. Falcon scanned the bobbing heads as she slipped into a space near the front. She saw Lily and Penny by the wall on the opposite side and waved. They didn't wave back. *I guess they can't see me with all the splashing,* she told herself.

As she went through the workout, jumping, kicking, and stretching to the sound of Frank's voice and the rhythms of BeauSoleil, she looked again at Lily and Penny. *I'll just casually start talking to them after class. Maybe we could all go shopping together.* She wished she had brought better clothes to change into. She strapped on a Styrofoam ankle weight.

*Lily is so gorgeous,* thought Falcon, *with those long legs and shiny black hair.* She contemplated her own short legs kicking up a fury of water as she lay on her back and held on to the edge of the pool. *I'm too short, and my hair is just . . . plain.* They had studied genetics in Human Biology, but as far as Falcon could see, she hadn't inherited anything from either of her parents. Toody's face looked just like Missy's, and his body was like the old photos of Peter in Aunt Emily's album. "If you look like anyone, my bird," said Missy, "it's Emily." Which was totally ridiculous since Great-Great-Aunt Emily was over a hundred years old. It's true that the first time Falcon had seen the pictures of Emily as a child, it had been like looking in a mirror. But Emily had been a beauty by the time she was thirteen, *and I for sure am NOT,* thought Falcon. She kicked even harder, as though she could make her legs grow longer by sheer force of will and water.

"Hey!" spluttered the woman next to her. "Are you trying

to drown me?" It was Allie Cadwallader-Newton's mother, grinning at her.

"Sorry," said Falcon.

Suddenly, to her horror, she felt solid coolness on her skin as the old green suit disintegrated under the strain of too many months of chlorine and kicking. She reached back to feel her bare bottom against the wall of the pool.

"What's wrong, Falcon?" asked Allie's mother. The rest of the class was moving to the center of the pool. Falcon blushed furiously.

"My bathing suit, it fell apart!" She almost hissed the words, near tears.

"Oh, lord. Okay, let's see. Don't move." Allie's mother pulled herself out of the pool, onto the side, and grabbed her towel.

"Falcon has a cramp. I'll take her out," she called to Frank, who had started over to see what was wrong. "It's okay, I've got her. You go on," she said. To Falcon's relief, Frank turned back to the class to lead some rather complicated exercises in the middle of the pool.

Ms. Cadwallader-Newton draped her big beach towel around Falcon's shoulders and pulled her out of the water, wrapping the towel around her as she stood up.

"There," she said, tucking in the end like a sarong. "Let's go. Can you limp?"

Falcon could and did, with Ms. Cadwallader-Newton's arm around her, back to the changing room. She was sure Lily and Penny had seen—she could feel their eyes like lasers on her back, seeing right through the towel to her bare butt, enormous and wobbling with fat as she hobbled away.

"Please, Ms. Cadwallader-Newton, don't tell Allie, OK? Don't tell anyone, please?"

Allie's mother crossed her heart. "Hope to die," she said.

At last they reached the safety of the changing room, and Falcon threw the remains of the treacherous bathing suit into the trash.

"You come with your little brother, don't you?" Ms. Cadwallader-Newton asked. "And your mother's an artist, isn't she? I think she knows my sister." Her voice came over the top of the changing room stall, where Falcon was pulling her clothes on as fast as she could.

"Yeah. I do. She is. Well, thank you for helping me and, you know, not telling or anything. I have to go now, OK? Bye." She was edging out of the changing room as she spoke.

"See you, Falcon," said Ms. Cadwallader-Newton as the door closed.

Falcon went to the Junior Swim room, remembering to limp. She sat on a bench to wait for Toody. She could see him practicing his crawl stroke with several other kids while Mei Chu directed them from the edge of the pool.

"Please, please, please don't let Lily and Penny have seen," she murmured to whatever gods might be listening. She hoped Allie's mother would keep her promise. Sometimes she ran into Allie with her weird brother at the museum or in the park. Falcon resolved to be extra nice to her next time so that in case her mother *had* told, Allie wouldn't spread it around. The thought of anyone finding out about her being practically naked in front of everyone made her shudder. *I'd die*, thought Falcon. *I would absolutely die.*

# CHAPTER TWO

FALCON HAD BEEN LOOKING FORWARD TO HAVING
dinner at Ardene's, but the feeling that the story of her
enormous bare butt was being whispered all over New York
City distracted her like an itch she couldn't scratch. She could
just see Penny's pointed, ratlike face telling it to an audience of
snickering kids.

Two years ago she would have gone straight up to 5A to
tell Ardene Taylor about the bathing suit. Ardene had been
Falcon's best grown-up friend for as long as she could remember. She and Missy had grown close in the last two years, and
they all had dinner together often. It was always fun, and Ardene, unlike Missy, was a great cook. Falcon thought about
telling her now, as they stood in the kitchen of 5A. Ardene was
dishing out portions of chocolate pudding cake while Falcon
spooned dollops of whipped cream on top.

"This has a ton of sugar and about a zillion calories, you

know," said Falcon. Ardene put the cake knife down and turned to stare at her, hands on hips.

"Falcon, are you really worried about calories?"

Falcon squirmed under Ardene's sharp brown gaze.

"Well, my butt is huge and I'm way too short, you know." She frowned at the plates of cake and cream, trying to ignore the smell of warm chocolate that filled the kitchen.

"Hmm," said Ardene. "Well, I don't think not eating dessert will make you any taller. But if you don't want cake, there's fruit in the fridge. Would you like a mango? They're very good."

"Uh, no thanks, I'll just have a little piece of this."

Ardene cut an inch-square piece of cake and handed the plate to Falcon. The cake looked lost on the glass dessert plate, and Falcon wished she hadn't said anything. She put a tiny blob of cream on the tiny piece of cake and went into the dining room. Missy didn't comment on Falcon's mingy dessert, but Toody took a huge bite of his own generous portion and said, "Hey! How come your piece is so small?"

"Don't talk with your mouth full, Tudor," said Missy, wiping a smear of chocolate sauce off the tablecloth in front of him.

Since it wasn't a school night, they stayed to play a game of Scrabble while Toody watched the Discovery Channel. Falcon hardly ever won because she cared more about forming interesting words than making a big score. Missy liked to invent words and try to convince everyone they were real.

"N-O-V-U-R-K-A, novurka," she said, setting down all seven tiles. "*And* triple word score, plus the 'r' on the end of 'quiddle,' that's a hundred and fifty-two points." She looked triumphant.

"Novurka? What does *that* mean?" asked Ardene, raising one eyebrow.

"It's a dance of intention," said Missy, pokerfaced. "A sort of prayer to ask God for something you want, only you dance it instead of saying it. It's, uh, Polish Orthodox."

"Uh-huh," said Ardene. "Falcon, will you look it up?" Missy's face fell.

Falcon dragged out the big dictionary and searched without success. "Novocain, novum, now," she muttered. "Nope. It's not here. Missy, were you cheating again?"

"It's not cheating," said Missy, holding on to her dignity with some difficulty. "It's . . . creative game strategy. *Somebody* has to invent new words."

As they walked back to 4B, Toody ran ahead to push the elevator button, and Falcon considered telling her mother about the pool.

After she had read Toody a story from *The Magical Monarch of Mo* and tucked him in, Missy came in to say goodnight to Falcon. She and Falcon had spent part of Christmas vacation painting the ceiling of Falcon's room midnight blue and sticking fluorescent paper stars all over it at random. The stars picked up light during the day and gave it off at night, so that in the dark Falcon could lie in bed and imagine she was looking up at the night sky.

"I really love this," said Missy, lying on her back across the bed and gazing up. "Maybe we could do my room during summer vacation."

Falcon lay back too and folded her arms under her head.

Looking up at the twinkly ceiling, she remembered a winter night two years ago.

"It reminds me of the night we—" Falcon stopped. *I'm not going to think about that,* she reminded herself.

"I wonder how she is," said Missy. "Your dragon, I mean."

"I never think about it. I'm too old for that magic stuff." She propped herself on one elbow and looked at her mother. "Anyhow, you don't even believe in it, you or Ardene either, remember? You said it wasn't real."

Missy sat up and crossed her legs.

"I know we did, little bird. Now I think we were wrong to . . . well, to lie to you. But I haven't forgotten that night. How could I? Egg was so beautiful, blazing against the snow, and you were so brave, my bird. Only we thought . . . we only meant . . . I'm sorry, Falcon."

Falcon tried to shut her mind to the thoughts that jangled and sparkled inside: dragons, witches, saints. And magic. She shut her eyes too, watching the colors flash behind her eyelids.

"Why?" she asked. "Why would you lie? And Ardene, too. It's so mean!" Two tears trickled down her cheeks, and she bit down hard on her lower lip to keep from crying.

"We didn't do it to be mean, truly, Falcon. I'm so sorry. I'm just so afraid sometimes." Missy put her hand on Falcon's forehead, the way she did when Falcon had a fever, and they sat silently for a while.

"It's time for you to talk to Emily," Missy said at last.

"But we just saw her last Sunday, like always. Aren't we going this Sunday too?"

"Not we. You. She's getting awfully old—we shouldn't have left it so long, but I was afraid. . . ."

"Why do you keep saying that? Afraid of *what*? And what do you mean, anyhow? She's always been old."

Missy smiled. "Even Emily was young once, Falcon. You know that; you've seen the pictures."

She had, but they didn't seem to have any connection to her great-great-aunt. Emily was over a hundred, and that was ancient.

"You still didn't say what you're so scared about," she said.

Missy stood up and straightened the covers on Falcon's bed. Henry appeared out of nowhere, jumped on the bed, turned around twice, and settled himself between Falcon's knees.

"I shouldn't have said that," said Missy. "It's only that . . . it's what mothers do, little bird. We worry. It's our job." She laughed, but the laugh sounded fake. Missy leaned over and kissed Falcon on the top of her head.

"You go talk to Emily on Sunday, and don't *you* worry. Sweet dreams." She was gone, closing the door partway so Henry could still get to his litter pan in the bathroom.

Falcon lay for a while staring up at the starry ceiling without seeing it. She didn't really want to go to Aunt Emily's alone. She hadn't seen her alone since she and Peter and Toody had flown home from Australia on the back of a . . . "NO!" she said, thumping her pillow and startling Henry. He leapt off the bed and stalked out of the room, his tail rigid with indignation. "No," she said again. "I won't think about that." That was all in the past, and the past was what her great-great-aunt would want to talk about. She always did.

Then she remembered her disintegrating bathing suit. She thought maybe she'd tell Aunt Emily about that, and about how worried she was that Lily and Penny had seen what had happened, and that Ms. Cadwallader-Newton would tell Allie, and. . . . She tossed in her bed, trying to beat the pillow into a comfortable shape. She wished Henry would come back; she wished someone would invent a tame pillow that stayed cool and smooth. And how could she be expected to sleep without Henry purring, with dragons on the ceiling in green bathing suits. . . .


Falcon didn't go to Waterobics on Saturday. She told her mother she had cramps, and Missy didn't question it. She just handed Falcon the hot-water bottle and gave her an absent-minded pat on the shoulder. Missy had just started working on a new book, *Wallaby for Rent,* and she vanished into her studio every day, right after breakfast. She always became even more scatterbrained than usual when she was doing the first draft of a book. She would leave the apartment without her wallet, go past her stop on the bus, wander around leaving things and forgetting where she'd put them. When the things were important, like house keys or royalty checks, she got hysterical. When the things were foods, as they often were, she made a mess. Falcon was always finding half-empty coffee cups gone slimy on the bookcases and moldy, half-eaten cheese sandwiches in the linen closet.

"Put Toody in a cab, would you, bird? And open a can of tuna or something for lunch. I'll be busy all day. Oh, and call

Emily, will you, so she'll know it's just you coming for elevenses? Now where did I put that yellow ochre? I had it a minute ago." She ambled off toward her studio at the back of the apartment, muttering to herself, with a coffee mug in one hand and the yellow ochre pencil behind her ear. Falcon knew she'd find it eventually, but not before she had sharpened a new one to use on the wallaby, whose name was Andrew. By evening her hair would be stuck full of colored pencils, her T-shirt would be stained with food and drawing ink, and she would either be silly and full of beans if the work had gone well, or silent and distracted if it hadn't.

Falcon put Toody in a cab and asked the driver to pick him up at eleven. Murray the doorman stuck his head in the cab. (Toody was great pals with all the building staff.)

"You swim to China, okay, sport?"

"I'm learning the strokeback," said Toody, demonstrating and nearly hitting Murray in the eye.

"He's a piece a work, your brother," said Murray, unwrapping a Snickers bar as the cab drove off. "Want half?"

"No thanks, I'm on a diet," said Falcon, heading for the elevator. She hadn't put any sugar on her cereal at breakfast and planned to buy skim milk when they went to the store tomorrow, after tea at Emily's. Then she remembered she was supposed to go to her great-great-aunt's alone and would have to call her. She hated talking to Emily on the phone. The old lady could hear pretty well face to face, but on the telephone you had to shout.

"Oh crap," she said, getting out on her floor and startling the elderly man who was stepping on.

"Sorry, Mr. Mott," she said. He ignored her, snapping the *Wall Street Journal* open with a loud crackle as the elevator doors closed.

"Stupid old fart," Falcon said, unlocking the door of 4B. She sighed. *I might as well get it over with,* she thought, and went into the kitchen. She sat on the counter with the phone and punched 1 on the speed dial. It rang eight times before the old lady picked up. It was always surprising how young her ancient aunt sounded when you couldn't see her.

"Hello?" she said.

"Aunt Emily, it's me, Falcon."

"Who is this?" Emily sounded annoyed. She hated people calling her up to sell her things or solicit money for worthy causes. "Worthy my foot!" she would say.

Falcon took a deep breath and screamed, "It's Falcon! Falcon Davies, your niece!"

"No need to shout, dear. I can hear you perfectly well. It's time we talked, you know. Will I see you tomorrow?"

"Yes, only not Toody and Missy. Just me."

"Well, of course I trust you, Falcon. Why wouldn't I?"

"No! JUST me. ONLY me. I'm coming alone." Falcon was gripping the phone so hard her hand ached. As usual, when she talked to Aunt Emily on the phone, she began to feel furious, as though the shouting itself made her angry.

"Lonely you indeed, my dear," said her aunt. "It's too bad you haven't found some friends at that school of yours."

"No, no! I said . . . oh, never mind. I'll see you tomorrow, okay?"

"Yes, dear, of course. Until then." Emily hung up, and Falcon sat slumped on the counter, exhausted. She got some apple juice and a bag of barbecue potato chips and went into the living room. She planned to curl up on the window seat with a new Frances M. Wood novel. Toody would be back in an hour and a half, but for now she was free.

Falcon did not, of course, have cramps. She had gotten her first period eight months before, but she wasn't regular at all. The bad part was that she never knew when to expect it. The good part was that she had a ready-made excuse anytime she wanted to get out of something. Missy, who had home remedies for practically everything, had a cure for cramps. It consisted of a hot-water bottle on your tummy, lots of hot tea, and the camel walk, where you walked around with your legs straight, your hands on the floor, and your butt in the air. This actually worked pretty well, except that the cramps came back as soon as you stood up. Nobody can walk around like that for very long.

In spite of the cramps, Falcon was kind of glad she'd finally gotten her period. She was almost the last girl in her class to get it, and she was beginning to think she never would. Bailey Jansen had gotten hers when she was ten, and practically all the girls had boobs except Falcon and Lily Weng. It was a good thing Lily didn't because it made it all right for Falcon to be flat-chested too.

She looked at herself in the mirror over the mantelpiece, arching her back to see if any boobs had popped up overnight. They hadn't. She couldn't see her butt in the mirror, but when she twisted around to look at it, it seemed huge, even after hardly any dessert last night and no sugar this morning.

Toody came back from Junior Swim in a roaring good mood and was perfectly happy to go into the TV room with a tuna sandwich, a bag of M&M's, and two Fred Astaire videos. Even with the door shut, Falcon could hear him clomping around. He had decided he was going to be an Olympic swimming and dancing champion, and he refused to listen when she told him the Olympics didn't include tap dancing.

Falcon returned to the window seat and *West to Madrugada*. Toody's voice was just barely audible from the TV room.

"Nightingale, you are the one," he sang, dancing around the room in unmatched socks while Fred Astaire danced on TV in impeccable evening clothes.

# CHAPTER THREE

W HEN FALCON WOKE UP ON SUNDAY, THE FIRST
thing she remembered was that she had to go to
Aunt Emily's by herself.

"It's not fair," she muttered, pulling on a cotton dress.
Aunt Emily liked them to be what she called "properly dressed"
for tea, morning or afternoon. Falcon looked in the full-length
mirror on the back of the closet door. The sleeveless dress was
made of unbleached cotton with a pattern of pale greens and
browns, and it actually looked pretty good. She twisted her
hair up off the back of her neck and anchored it with a tor-
toiseshell barrette. *I should pay more attention to how I look*, she
thought. *And to boys.* Lily and Penny were always whispering
about which boys were "hot." Falcon wasn't exactly sure what
hot was or how a person got to be that way, but she was deter-
mined to find out. Missy came in as she was hunting for her
sandal under the bed.

"Oh, bird, you look really pretty. You want a squirt of Summer Magic?" Summer Magic was Missy's latest homemade perfume, a combination of lemon, attar of roses, and vetivert. Falcon thought it smelled like furniture polish. She dodged her mother's spray bottle.

"No thanks. I just took a shower." This wasn't exactly true, but she'd had one the day before and had checked her armpits for stinkiness and put on clean underwear. Swimming every day gave her skin a faint, permanent smell of chlorine that she liked much better than Summer Magic.

Missy was wearing baggy blue shorts with hiking boots. She looked so strange that Falcon was glad they wouldn't be together.

"We're going to see the throwing-up people at the museem," said Toody as he walked in, carrying a piece of toast. That explained the hiking boots. Missy liked serious shoes for museum walking.

The throwing-up people were part of a little clay village in the Central American wing of the American Museum of Natural History. At the moment they were Toody's favorites. Falcon knew that after they saw them, he and Missy would walk around the park pretending to throw up, a second reason to be glad she was going to Emily's instead.

"You're getting jelly on the floor," Falcon said.

Toody squatted down, scooped up the blob with his finger, and put it in his mouth.

"Oh gross! Missy, can't you make him not do that?"

"Too late now," said her mother. "And as Gammy Tudge says, 'Us is all got to eat a peck o' dirt afore us dies.'"

Falcon couldn't help laughing. Gammy Tudge was a

made-up old woman from the country who said wise things. Or they were supposed to be wise. Falcon didn't know who had invented Gammy, but she was pretty sure it was Missy.

"I'd like to know just exactly *what* country she's supposed to be from," Peter had said.

"Oh you know, *the* country. Cows, hay, butter churns," said Missy, waving a hand in the air to conjure up rural visions. "Olden times."

Remembering that reminded Falcon that her father was in town. Peter was in New York a lot lately. She thought she'd ask him if they could have a day alone together during the week.

They left the apartment, Missy and Toody going across 77th Street to the museum and Falcon heading for the crosstown bus at West 65th Street.

"We're having Mexican takeout with Freddy Maldonado tonight, Falcon. Around six, if you want to come," said Missy as they parted.

"Okay, I'll see," said Falcon, leaving them at the entrance to the museum and walking down to the corner of 65th Street and Central Park West. She decided she definitely would not go to Freddy's, though she liked him quite a lot. But his rooms in the southeast tower of the museum were packed too full of memories. Memories of dragons and magic. She needed to forget all that and focus on more important things.

As soon as Falcon turned the corner she stopped, leaned against a railing, and pulled a lipstick and small mirror out of her fanny pack. When she had finished painting her mouth with Midnight Shimmer, she was sure she looked at least sixteen. Even without any boobs.

As she boarded the bus the driver smiled and said, "Need a transfer, princess?"

"No, thank you," she said haughtily. He was really old, at least thirty, and the uniform he wore was hopelessly dorky. She was absolutely sure that bus drivers were *not* hot. To avoid him she walked up the aisle and took a seat in the middle instead of her favorite one at the front, where she could put her feet up on the bulge over the wheel and get the best view of the park.

"Falcon?" It was Allie Cadwallader-Newton, and she was wearing a floppy cloth hat so large that the brim brushed her shoulders, a long-sleeved shirt, and pants even floppier than the hat. *In a way,* thought Falcon, *you have to admire someone who goes around dressed like that and doesn't care what people think.* Then she looked around the bus to make sure nobody she knew would see her talking to such a geek.

Allie turned to face Falcon and pushed the hat off her head, letting it dangle by the cord that anchored it under her chin.

"Skin cancer," she said.

"What?" Falcon asked.

"Skin cancer. You get it from the sun. Especially redheads with pale skin, like me and Fig. Well, my whole family actually. My dad had to have a cancer spot removed from his nose."

"Oh," said Falcon, wondering what Allie's father would look like with part of his nose gone. It made a picture in her mind she didn't want to look at. She remembered that she had to be extra nice to Allie in case her mother had told her about what had happened at the pool.

"So, uh, where are you going?" The bus was winding through the part of the park where the trees were so lush that the branches almost met overhead, and the smell of the air coming through the open windows was as cool and green as leaf shade.

"The zoo. I like to sit in the penguin house. Oh, and the polar bears. I love their feet."

"Me too!" said Falcon, forgetting for a moment that the zoo was for babies and she was trying to be one of the cool kids. "When they push off against the glass wall of their pool, those furry pads, they look like humongous bedroom slippers!"

"Yes," said Allie, "and their bottoms are so round and big."

Falcon squinted at her suspiciously. Was that a hint about her own enormous bare bottom?

"What do you mean?" she asked. Allie didn't notice the coldness in Falcon's voice. She propped her chin on her folded arms over the back of the seat.

"When they push off," she said, "with those feet, and their bottoms and bellies are so round and fuzzy, they look soooooo happy, like—" She stretched out her arms and let her face relax into an expression of idiotic bliss. *"Whoosh!"* She collapsed into a fit of laughter so contagious that Falcon couldn't help joining her. She remembered that Allie was only eleven and three quarters, having skipped the first grade. *She's just a kid,* thought Falcon. *Maybe she didn't mean anything.*

"You want to come too?" asked Allie. She had always wanted to get to know Falcon, particularly now that she and her brother, Fig, weren't as close as they used to be.

"I can't," said Falcon sadly, to her own surprise. She would have liked to join Allie at the zoo, especially at this early hour, before it was mobbed by people with small children hanging on to their hands.

"I have to go see my great-great-aunt. Um, maybe you could come too? We could go to the zoo after and get a hot dog."

"It'll be crowded by then," said Allie. "Anyhow, won't your aunt mind?"

"Oh no, she'd like it," said Falcon, who actually had no idea whether Emily would mind or not. Her aunt had said she wanted to talk to her, and in Falcon's experience, when a grownup used the word *talk* in that way, with invisible quotation marks around it, *talk* usually meant *lecture*. She would be very happy to avoid that and get on Allie's good side at the same time.

"She's a cool lady, my aunt Emily. She's over a hundred but she's super smart and she knew everybody famous." Then Falcon remembered that the famous people Emily had known were all dead, and probably Allie wouldn't have heard of them anyway. When she told Lily and Penny that Emily had known Teddy Roosevelt and Nijinsky, they said, "Who?" Allie, however, seemed impressed by Aunt Emily's age alone.

"A hundred!" she said, her blue eyes growing enormous. The oldest person she'd ever met was Mr. Gottlieb who owned the Sutton Place Deli, and he was only eighty-seven.

"*Over* a hundred," said Falcon. She remembered that Allie's aunt was an artist. "Aunt Emily knew all these famous artists, like Picasso and—" Before she could say another word, Allie grabbed her arm over the back of the seat.

"PICASSO!" squealed Allie, her voice rising into an almost inaudible squeak, like a bat's. "Your aunt actually knew *Pablo Picasso?!*" For a moment Falcon wondered whether her aunt had known the right Picasso. What if it was Joe Picasso or Fred Picasso waving in that old photograph?

"Uh, yeah, sure. *The* Picasso, the artist," she said. The bus stopped on East 68th Street at Fifth Avenue, and she moved toward the door, pulling Allie, who was so excited she nearly fell down the steps. They walked toward Aunt Emily's building on the corner of 66th Street. Allie couldn't stop talking.

"Omigosh," she said, "I'm going to meet someone who actually knew Picasso! Are you really sure it's okay, Falcon? I mean, I'm not invited or anything; won't she mind?"

"She'll love it," said Falcon, trying to steer Allie, who was chattering about Picasso and weaving all over the sidewalk. The doorman nodded at Falcon as they walked into Aunt Emily's apartment building.

"She's expecting you. Go right on up," he said. As usual, Aunt Emily took a long time to answer the door. When she opened it, she leaned forward on her silver-topped cane and peered at Falcon.

"If your mouth were really that color, I'd call 911. And who is this?" she asked. She smiled up at Allie, who gazed in awe at the old lady.

"I'm Alice Cadwallader-Newton, ma'am," she said, and then she did something that actually looked like a curtsy. Aunt Emily looked astonished.

"Well!" she said, "I'm delighted to meet you, my dear. Do come in. Ana has made the most delicious blueberry corn cake for our elevenses. I'm sure you've had no breakfast, Falcon, so, if you'd like, she can scramble some eggs for you as well."

"Just cake'll be fine," said Falcon. Allie was standing speechless before a small painting hanging in the foyer. It showed a woman handing a bowl to a child.

"It's real, isn't it?" she asked, whispering as though she were in church. "That's an actual Picasso; you have a real Picasso right here . . . Omigosh." She stared at the painting as hard as she could, trying to photograph it with her eyes so she could describe it exactly to her aunt Bijou. Bijou was an artist, and she said Picasso was "one of the giants."

"Indeed I do," said Aunt Emily, "and there's a pen-and-ink sketch by him in my bedroom, and a Matisse in the dining room, if you like his work too. Falcon, why don't you run into the kitchen and help Ana. I'll take your friend on a little tour." She led an enraptured Allie into the dining room.

Falcon went into the kitchen, where Ana, Aunt Emily's maid, was dusting a cake with powdered sugar. Ana had been with Emily for as long as Falcon could remember. She had come from Argentina forty years before, and when Falcon was little, Ana used to baby-sit from time to time. She was a tall, big woman with a mane of black and silver hair that she kept coiled in a braided bun at the back of her neck, and she had long, skinny legs like a stork under the skirt of her gray uniform. She used to come in just three times a week, to clean and do a little cooking, but now, with her own children grown and Emily getting so old and frail, she came every day. Ana and Emily usually spoke Spanish together, and she had taught Falcon a few phrases.

*"Ola, Falcon,"* said Ana. *"¿Y como estas?"*

*"Bien, gracias, Ana. ¿Y usted?"* said Falcon. It was hard to make her tongue do Spanish when it had been doing English all week. Spanish gives your tongue a lot of exercise because of the r's.

"Paint," said Ana, switching suddenly to English. "You are too young for painting your face." She handed Falcon a paper towel.

When Missy had told her she couldn't wear makeup till she was fifteen, Falcon was outraged, but somehow it didn't bother her coming from Ana. She wiped off the Midnight Shimmer and helped herself to a blueberry from the crystal bowl Ana was setting on a tray. Ana added a silver sugar bowl, milk jug, and tea strainer and handed the tray to Falcon. She carried it into the living room, where Aunt Emily was showing Allie the album that contained a photograph of Picasso, standing behind a much younger Emily in a café in Paris.

"He was a dangerous man in his way," Emily was saying. "Artists often are, you know. They're supposed to be. Artists, writers, actors, singers, dancers . . . anyone who is passionate about his work. Or her work. Though most women, even now, seem to feel the pull of family more than men do."

"But why was he dangerous?" asked Allie. She was completely absorbed in Aunt Emily and her stories and hardly noticed as Falcon set the tray down and sat on her aunt's other side. Falcon looked for the thousandth time at the black-and-white snapshot of people frozen by a camera at a Paris café in 1933.

"You can't tell by that photograph," said Emily, "but he was so attractive. When he wanted to, he could make you think you were the most beautiful and charming creature in the world. People—men and women both—would do anything for him. In truth he didn't care about anyone much, not for more than a minute. He often treated people very badly."

Falcon wondered how anyone could think the short, grinning man in the picture was attractive. Allie was touching the snapshot reverently with her finger, wishing she could go back in time and have a café au lait with Picasso himself.

"I never knew he was a bad person," she said. "I wish I didn't know it now."

"I didn't say he was bad," said Emily. "He was no worse than a lot of people. Most people behave badly sometimes, and most of them are not great artists. Pablo was."

"You mean," said Falcon, thinking of Missy, "it's okay to hurt people if you're an artist?" She wasn't sure whether her mother was a great artist or not. She was certainly not a great mother.

"No, of course not, Falcon," said Emily. "It's only that, unless you are one of the people getting hurt, that's not what really matters in the long run. What matters is the work."

Allie's face had turned bright pink. Watching her, it occurred to Falcon that Allie's pale skin was like a barometer of her moods. It turned pink or red every time she felt something strongly. Sometimes it was just patches on her cheeks; sometimes it colored her whole face, as it did now.

"Oh, no!" cried Allie. "Excuse me, Ms. Davies, but I don't think that's right. People, people's feelings, do matter. They must."

Falcon remembered a sort of riddle her father had once asked her.

"Peter says, if you were in a shipwreck and there was only room in the lifeboat for one person besides yourself, would you choose a baby, Mother Teresa, your own mother, or William Shakespeare?"

Allie's eyes widened. "Oh," she said. "Oh, well, my moth— or, no, the ba—of course, Mother Teresa and William Shakespeare if they weren't dead, though wouldn't there really be room for another person? They could hold the baby. Maybe some people could sort of hold on to the lifeboat and, you know, take turns being in it while other people were in the water?" She didn't like the idea of being in a lifeboat. She had seen the movie about the *Titanic* and still had nightmares about those people in the dark, freezing water, screaming.

Aunt Emily said, "I think it would depend on whether Mr. Shakespeare had already written his plays and sonnets. If he had, I'd let him drown."

"What about the others?" asked Falcon.

"Yes, and what about your mother?" asked Allie.

"My mother was a perfectly dreadful woman, and I've always thought Mother Teresa must have been an awful pill. As for babies, well, I don't care for them at all. Drown 'em all, I say! *Glug, glug, glug.*" There was a mischievous look on her face that reminded Falcon of Toody.

Falcon snorted with laughter as much at the shocked expression on Allie's face as at her aunt. After a moment, Allie laughed too. Falcon's great-great-aunt wasn't anything like what she thought such an old person would be like. She turned to Falcon.

"Peter's your father, isn't he? What does *he* say the right answer is?"

"He says he'd drown them all and save the ship's cat. And there isn't a right answer."

"They're rather like dragons," said Emily, who was staring thoughtfully into space. This remark made no sense, and not for the first time Falcon wondered whether her aunt had Alzheimer's. She often said things that seemed to come out of nowhere. Falcon had asked Missy about it not long ago.

"I don't think so, bird. I've known her since I met your father, when we were only ten years old, and she's always been that way. Of course she was already in her seventies then. I don't know, really." Missy frowned and began to chew her left thumbnail. "I don't like to think about her getting old, and . . . I really don't want to talk about it."

Falcon didn't like to think about it either, but it was silly to talk about Emily *getting* old; her great-great-aunt *was* old, older than practically anybody. Allie wasn't at all puzzled by Emily's dragon remark. She nodded her head.

"Yes," she said, "I see what you mean, because they're dangerous too, but also sort of . . ."

"Splendid," said Emily. "Splendid and powerful, but dangerous."

"What are you talking about?" asked Falcon. It was very annoying to have a complete stranger understand her aunt better than she did.

"Artists," said Allie. "Artists, writers, that kind of person being dangerous. And also magical, like dragons are." She was suddenly hungry and took a big bite of blueberry corn cake, which she had forgotten until now. Falcon, who had eaten two pieces, noticed with envy how skinny she was.

"Good," said Allie, washing the cake down with milky tea. "That's really good cake."

"Ana is a genius at baking. You must tell her you liked it— she'll be so pleased. It's a shame huckleberries are so scarce these days; they're far more delicious than these cultivated blueberries." Aunt Emily paused, and Falcon saw a familiar look on her face. *Oh no!* she thought. She knew exactly what her aunt was going to do. It was *so* lucky that Allie was here and not Lily Weng. She would have died if it had been Lily. Even so, she cringed as Emily clapped her hands and began to sing.

"H-U-uckle-uckle, B-U-buckle-buckle, that spells huckle-berry PIE!"

Allie looked thunderstruck and then burst out laughing. Emily looked pleased. Falcon glared at Allie. Allie felt pleas-antly floppy, the way you do after a really good laugh.

"Oh, that's funny!" she said. "Did you make that up, Ms. Davies?"

"No," said Emily. "I heard it many years ago, in a variety show. D'you know, I've always wished I had gone on the stage myself. It's one of the few things I haven't done. My song did not amuse you, Falcon. I saw you rolling your eyes."

"I did think it was funny the *first* time," said Falcon. Emily turned to Allie.

"But you, my dear, tell me, are you familiar with dragons,

or magic?" She put on the wire-rimmed glasses that hung from a cord around her neck and focused her pale eyes on Allie's face.

The conversation had quite suddenly taken a turn that made Falcon extremely nervous, as though the word *dragon* had opened a door she thought was locked. She tried to change the subject.

"I'm learning to cook, Aunt Emily. You know Missy doesn't like to, so I got this cookbook, *The Joy of*—"

"Yes, yes," said Emily, waving *The Joy of Cooking* away with a blue-veined hand. "You were saying, Allie, about dragons?"

"I've never actually seen one," said Allie, rolling a blueberry around her plate with one finger. "But I've always wondered about, well, not only dragons, but all those things, you know? Witches and sorcerers? Magic? Then last year . . ." Her cheeks were bright pink again, and she was slightly breathless. She had never talked about this to anyone but her brother. But somehow she thought she could trust Falcon and Aunt Emily to listen, and to believe. She spoke slowly, remembering.

"My brother and I, we're twins, and we were at the natural history museum, and we sort of got . . . whirled out of time through a diorama."

"Did you indeed, my dear. How very extraordinary." Aunt Emily no longer looked the least bit vague. In fact, she looked wide awake and somehow younger. Much younger. Now it was Allie who stared into space as the memories unrolled in her mind, like a film.

"We went back to 1913 first, in France, and then . . ." A shadow of fear crossed her face, and she shuddered. "The Ice Age—we went there and stayed a long time. We couldn't get back till the shaman helped us. He was stuck in time too. He was an artist. He painted the diorama that whirled us, Quigley did. That was his name."

"Quigley? Not Hieronymous Quigley?" said Emily, half jumping out of her chair. Like Allie, her face was flushed and her eyes glittered with excitement.

"Yes, Hieronymous," said Allie, staring at the old lady and wondering if she'd said something wrong.

"Hieronymous Quigley, good heavens! Now, my dear, calm yourself, have more tea, more cake, and just tell us the rest, if you would. This is really quite extraordinary—Quigley, that rascal! Who'd've thought?"

In Falcon's opinion, it was Aunt Emily who needed calming more than Allie. She was breathing hard, pouring tea into Allie's cup with a shaking hand so that it slopped into the saucer. She didn't even notice the mess but set the pot down and seized Allie's arm.

"How, my dear, just exactly *how* did you do it?"

Allie, who until now had been enjoying Aunt Emily's company very much, shrank back against the sofa cushions, trying to pull her arm out of the old lady's surprisingly strong grip. She gulped.

"Do what?"

"Time travel, of course," said Falcon's aunt, giving Allie's arm a shake and then dropping it. To Allie's relief, Emily had calmed down and seemed to be in control again. She poured herself a cup of tea with a perfectly steady hand, added a slice of lemon, and took a long swallow.

"Now then," she said. "Tell us all about it."

"I don't exactly know, Ms. Davies. All the times Fig and I did it we span. Spun. But Mr. Quigley didn't; he just jumped. Fig said time was like a series of carousels all spinning at once, and you had to jump on at just the right time. But we never found out how to tell when the right time was."

"Spinning. Well, of all things," said Emily. "Who would have thought? And Quigley of all people. We always wondered what had happened to him. We got together, you know, some of us who thought he was a kind of genius, and we paid off his creditors, thinking that when he heard about it, he'd come back. But, of course, he never did."

Falcon chewed on a hangnail, wishing she had never invited Allie to Emily's house. *Time travel sounds a lot like magic,* she thought. *I can't get away from it.*

# CHAPTER FOUR

F ALCON HAD HAD THIS FEELING BEFORE, OF BEING just on the edge of panic while one part of her brain continued to function with perfect clarity. Now it was that clear part that reminded her of the time two years ago when she had jumped into a pool to save Toody from drowning. She remembered how he sank to the bottom as she tried again and again to get her arms around his small, slippery body. That near disaster had been her fault. Now Allie's story of whirling through time made her dizzy, and it was her fault for bringing Allie here in the first place. *I hate this stuff, this magic,* she fumed, *and it's my fault, it's always my fault, there must be something really wrong with me . . .*

Allie finished her second piece of cake and gulped the last of her cold tea. It felt good to let the secret out. She knew her parents and her aunt had never really believed it, and they never wanted to talk about it.

*She seems perfectly calm now too,* thought Falcon. *I'm the one being pulled into this, this MESS, this—*

"Magic," she said, not realizing she had spoken aloud.

"Just so," said Emily. "You know, it's especially propitious, you girls coming here today. It's the twenty-second of April, the eve of St. George's Day, the day I first saw the dragons, and the day almost a century later when Falcon found Egg. And that brings me to what I wanted to talk to you about, my dear. Ordinarily I wouldn't discuss it in front of a stranger, but I think . . ." She smiled at Allie and patted her knee. "I think perhaps your friend here may be one of us."

"Us?" said Falcon. "One of us who?"

"Magnets. The Davies. The Penrys, the Lloyds, the Glendowers, and the Cadwalladers too, some of them. Of course, most of them are perfectly ordinary. But every few generations there is one who is different, and special. I am one, you are, of course, and I do believe that Allie may be too. I don't know about her brother. Most of us are women, though not all, by no means all. King Arthur himself, he was a powerful Magnet, poor man, and so was da Vinci—now he . . ."

Allie was listening hard to what Aunt Emily was saying. *Why did she say it's me and maybe not my brother? Maybe that's why Fig and I can't talk like we used to. He still seems like a little kid and I . . . What am I? Did she really see dragons? And what is Egg? What does she mean?*

"What do you mean? What are you talking about?" Falcon clenched her fists, rigid with fury. Allie's mouth hung slightly open. *She looks like a fish,* thought Falcon, who wanted to slap them both.

"Really, my dear, you must let me tell this in my own way," said Emily. "No need to become so overwrought. Shall I ask Ana to make more tea?"

"No! I mean, no thank you. I'm fine." Falcon took a deep breath. "I'm listening."

"That's good, to breathe like that," said Allie. "My mother says . . . oh. Sorry, Ms. Davies." Aunt Emily waited for silence, as any good storyteller must.

"As I was saying," she said, "we are Magnets. Magnets for magic and for the world of magic. I mean, all those things you've wondered about, Allie: witches, dragons, sorcerers, elves and fairies, goblins, trolls, all of them. All the world that lives just outside the light of a hearth fire. It's been there since long before there *were* hearth fires, and now, well, I suppose the hearth fire is Science. Magic is all the things we don't understand. Science has explained some of them, which isn't quite the same as understanding."

"Like the people who would have captured Egg, and . . . dissected her." Falcon gulped, remembering the armed mob around her beloved dragon. "Is that what you mean?"

"Partly. Of course, most of those people weren't scientists. They were just greedy to exploit Egg for money. But it's true that sometimes a researcher will do harm in the name of science. Even supposing they could, no one should dissect a dragon." Ana, without being asked, came in just then with a fresh pot of tea and handed Aunt Emily a glass of water and a small blue pill.

"*Su píldora, Señora Davies.* It is time for your pill. Falcon, I am going to the store, but I have made soup and sandwiches if you and Alice will stay for lunch."

"*Gracias, Ana, hasta luego,*" said Emily, taking a sip of the water.

"*La píldora,*" said Ana. She folded her arms and waited until Emily put the pill in her mouth and swallowed.

"*Hasta luego,*" she said, and smiled at the two girls. "Falcon, Alice, *adiós.*" She left the room, and they heard the hall door open and shut.

As soon as the door closed behind Ana, Aunt Emily took the pill out of her mouth and wrapped it in a Kleenex.

"Aunt Emily, you shouldn't . . ."

"Falcon, I am quite old enough to decide what I should or shouldn't do. Those pills make me woozy. Now then, where was I?"

"Not dissecting dragons," said Allie, looking worried as she stared at the blue-stained Kleenex. She wished Aunt Emily had swallowed the pill. *If she's over a hundred, she probably really needs it,* she thought.

"Ah yes. Well, that's part of what we do, we Magnets. We protect the magic creatures and places from those who would harm them, whether out of fear or misdirected curiosity—it doesn't matter. We have no magical powers ourselves, really, except for a greater ability to . . . to pay attention than most people. We see the green elf peeking out from a bush, the saint under the ragged clothing, the glow of a dragon's egg in Central Park. Or the possibilities behind the glass of a museum diorama."

She smiled at them both and took Falcon's hand.

"You are thirteen, Falcon, so it's high time you knew who and what you are. You too, Allie. Your mother is probably the one who would have told you, and soon. Cadwallader is one of the names, one of *our* names."

"Missy and Peter, are they . . . ?" asked Falcon, thinking that her parents had both seen dragons, and that Peter had seen much more: a witch and a saint.

"They're not, but they know about you. Peter has known about me all his life. He was not surprised to have a daughter who is a Magnet. But Missy, it terrifies her, and she worries about you. She's afraid for you."

Allie moved closer to Aunt Emily, magical visions filling her mind.

"Oh, Ms. Davies, do you mean that I'm a Magnet too, that I'll see more magic, maybe even a dragon or a witch?"

Aunt Emily cupped her hand against Allie's cheek.

"It seems you are, my dear. So, there are three of us all together in this room. It's an extraordinary coincidence. Or perhaps, not a coincidence at all."

Allie leapt up and began to dance around the room, singing, "Witches and dragons and elves, oh my! Witches and dragons and elves, oh my!"

Falcon glared at her, and at her aunt, who was watching with great amusement. She would have liked to pull Allie's red hair till she screamed. Emily's news was like a heavy cloak she would be forced to wear, even though it was much too big for her, even though she didn't want to wear it. Lily and Penny, their world of clothes and forbidden pleasures, the freedom, excitement, and power of being one of the cool kids seemed far away and infinitely desirable.

"Aunt Emily," Falcon said. The old lady was still watching Allie dance, swaying and humming along.

"AUNT EMILY!" Falcon shouted, seizing her aunt's skinny old arm.

"Yes, yes, Falcon, what is it? I'm not deaf, you know." The old woman sounded irritated, and Falcon thought, *Yes you are, you are deaf, and you don't listen to me, you're so full of magical this and mystical that and Allie acting like a total weirdo and all that dragon CRAP!*

"I don't want to be what you said. A magnet for magic. I want to be . . . just a person, a regular, ordinary person like everybody else."

Allie stopped dancing and dropped, flushed and breathless, onto the pink velvet armchair that Falcon always thought of as Aunt Emily's throne. Emily stared at her niece and at the chewed fingernails on the hand that gripped her arm. After a long moment she pulled away and spoke in a voice that sounded old and very tired.

"Well, my dear, of course that is up to you. You are what you are and nothing can change that, but what you do, how you live your life, that is yours to choose. I suppose it is natural for you to try on different personalities at your age, but I must say I find this one singularly unpleasant." She stood up, leaning heavily on her cane. All the years of her long life seemed to drag at her body, which suddenly looked terribly thin and frail.

"Be careful, Falcon, about denying this gift you have, this . . . talent. It may harm you if you don't use it. I am going to have my nap now. Do help yourselves to Ana's luncheon. She would be so pleased to know you enjoyed it." She reached out to Allie, who scrambled up from her chair and took Emily's hand, wishing she could take the hurt look off the old woman's face.

"Thank you!" Allie said. "So much. It's been . . ." She couldn't find words.

"Goodbye, Allie, I'm so glad we've met. I hope we can—" Suddenly she cried out and crumpled to the floor, clutching her chest. Allie and Falcon bent over her, trying to understand her strangled whisper.

"Pill. Handbag . . . " They looked frantically around the room but saw no handbag nor any pills.

"Nine-one-one," said Allie. "Where's the phone?" Falcon ran to the phone in the hall and dialed, forcing herself to speak calmly to the bored voice at the other end.

"Is he breathing?" it said.

"She! Yes, but hardly at all, and her lips are blue."

"Address, please."

Falcon gave the address while she stared into the living room. Her view of Emily was partly blocked by the back of the sofa. She could see Allie cradling the old lady in her arms.

"Sixty-fifth Street. Okay, they're on the way."

"NO! NO! NO! Sixty-sixth Street—six six—oh, please hurry!"

The line went dead.

She pushed redial to make sure the ambulance had the right address, but all she got was a busy signal. She slammed the phone down and ran into the living room.

Allie looked up, her face pale.

"Oh, Falcon, I think she's . . . she's barely breathing."

"Shush! She's trying to say something." Falcon leaned over her aunt, trying to hear.

"Pin . . . pin . . ." Her lips barely moved; the words were scarcely more than a puff of air.

"Pill? You want the pill? Where's your bag, Aunt Emily?"

Emily panted, unable to catch her breath. Her eyes were desperate as she summoned all her remaining strength.

"Sssspin. Take. Me. Past. Now." Her head fell back.

"What?" asked Falcon. "What did she say?"

All at once Allie understood what Emily was trying to say. She jumped to her feet and slid her arms under the old lady's.

"What are you doing? Stop that! You'll kill her!" Falcon grabbed at Allie, who was lifting Emily's shoulders off the floor.

"Stop it! Help me, Falcon! Take her feet! Don't you see, she said SPIN! She wants us to spin her back to before this happened!"

"Are you crazy? Let her go, you stupid, you're killing her!" The girls struggled, pulling Aunt Emily between them like a rag doll.

Then, out of nowhere, came a chorus of voices, crashing and echoing around the room to the sound of a thousand tiny bells:

"SPIN!" said a pretty good witch.

"SPIN!" came the bass rumble of an ancient dragon.

"SPIN, I SAY, SPIN!" said a saint in Reeboks and a battered halo.

"SPIN, MY FIRST FRIEND, SPIN!" said Egg, burning and blazing.

Sobbing, Falcon bent down and took Aunt Emily's ankles in her hands. Her skin felt clammy and cold and her hundred pounds were a dead weight between the two girls. They turned slowly, awkwardly at first, but as they found the rhythm they circled faster and faster as a thin gray mist rose around them. The shapes of the living room furniture grew blurry, while the Persian rug beneath their feet became a whirling kaleidoscope of color.

The mist swirled around them as they spun, the centrifugal force so strong that Falcon feared Aunt Emily would be torn in two by its pull.

# CHAPTER FIVE

GRADUALLY THEY BEGAN TO SLOW DOWN. THEY heard jangling, rumbling sounds and smelled wood smoke and wisteria and . . .

"Horse manure," said Allie, stumbling as they landed with a bump on a plot of grass.

As their vision cleared, Falcon and Allie saw that they were in a small garden in front of a brownstone house opposite Gramercy Park. Between them a young girl struggled to free herself from their hands.

"Let me go!" she said and stood up. She had straight brown hair in a long braid tied with a big, rather bedraggled bow, and she wore a blue dress with a white sailor collar, thick black stockings, and black kid boots that went halfway up her legs.

"Here's a pretty howde doo!" said the girl. "If you don't close your mouths, the flies'll fly in."

It couldn't be, but it was.

"Uh, uh, Aunt Emily?" said Falcon.

"Great-Great-Aunt Emily to you, young lady," said the girl, and she exploded with laughter at the look on Falcon's face.

"Where are we? I mean, *when* are we?" asked Allie.

Aunt Emily looked around at the garden and the tall brownstone house and then down at herself. She straightened the bow in her hair and cleaned the mud off her boots by rubbing them on the backs of her legs. She balanced easily on one foot, right then left, in turn. It didn't improve the boots, and it made the stockings much worse.

"Nineteen-oh-three I'd say, or thereabouts, which makes me about twelve." She jumped up and down a few times. "I feel perfectly wonderful!" Her voice was slightly higher than it had been when she was old, but there was no doubt about who it was.

Allie laughed and took the hands that felt so different from the bony old claws she had held only a moment before. These were smooth and strong and full of life.

"I'm so glad you're alive!" she said. She looked more closely at the girl, and then at Falcon.

"You know, you two look so much alike you could almost be twins—well, sisters anyhow." It was true. As Falcon studied Emily she could see the resemblance even more than before.

"I'm taller," she said, but really it was only a matter of an inch or so. "And I'm much more mature. I have boobs."

Emily stuck out her flat chest. "Bosoms!" she said. "No, you don't either." Her face twisted for a moment and she said, "A dreadful word, Falcon, quite vulgar. But I'm glad I'm alive too, Allie. Very glad indeed!"

"Fine," said Falcon. "Fine. Let's all be glad. Here we are,

trapped in 1903 with no way to get home, so let's just laugh and dance around and be glad."

"Falcon," said Emily, "if you would rather I were dead, or lying in a hospital stuck full of needles and tubes, I'm sorry. But I am glad I'm not, and as for being trapped, we don't know that we are. After all, Allie came all the way back from the Ice Age. We have only a hundred years to go."

Falcon squirmed under her aunt's calm gray gaze. *After all, it's my fault she had the heart attack.* To avoid thinking about that, she looked around. The people strolling by on the sidewalk stared back at her in her flimsy sundress, bare legs, and sandals, and at Allie's baggy pants. Children laughed and pointed, while the grownups looked away and said things like, "Outrageous! Disgraceful! It shouldn't be allowed!"

All at once Emily's face seemed to go out of focus and grimaced as though she were in pain.

"Get out! Get out of my head this minute!"

Emily's face was writhing horribly, and Falcon wondered if she was having another heart attack. She stepped toward her just as Emily lashed out with her fists, catching Falcon on the cheek with such violence that she fell to the ground.

"Hey!" she cried. Allie dodged the flying fists and grabbed Emily's wrists.

"Stop it! It is you, Ms. Davies—you are in there, aren't you?"

Emily was red-faced and panting.

"Yes," said Aunt Emily. "We *both* are, me and . . ."

"Me!" cried a furious voice. Falcon and Allie stared at the girl, who seemed to have calmed down a bit.

46

"I'm in here with myself at twelve years old, together in the same body." Aunt Emily sounded shaky, as though she were struggling to control herself. "The same brain."

"You have to leave right now," said Young Emily. "There's no room. It hurts. Please go." She hiccupped and brushed her hand across her eyes. "I'm *not* crying," she said, scowling. She took a deep breath, turned on her heel, and marched toward the house.

"Come along," she said over her shoulder. "My governess will fix it."

"Yes!" said Aunt Emily. "That's it. Blinda's here, we'll ask her." She (or they) walked up the steps, with Falcon and Allie trailing behind. Emily rang the bell, and the door was opened by a man in a black suit whose eyes widened only slightly at the sight of Falcon and Allie in their peculiar clothes.

"Thank you, Graves," said Young Emily. "Where is my governess?"

"I believe she is in the schoolroom, Miss Emily." Emily led them up two flights of stairs and down a long hall. She flung open a door and ushered them into a large, sunny room lined with books. There was a table in the middle with four chairs around it. Two easels stood by the windows, and two armchairs with a small table between them sat before a fireplace where a coal fire burned. A plump, pink-cheeked woman sat in one of the armchairs, reading a copy of the *Saturday Evening Post*. She looked up when they entered and Falcon saw, to her astonishment, that it was her old friend Blinda Cholmondely, the Charles Street Witch.

"Ah, Emily, good. I was just going to fetch you for your French lesson. Well! And who are your friends, may I ask?" Her face was friendlier than her words, and Allie had the feeling that she was playing the part of a strict and proper person rather than actually being one.

"Blinda!" said Falcon. "I'm so glad you're here! We're in a terrible mess." Blinda stared at her with a puzzled expression.

"I'm quite sure we haven't met," she said. "And yet . . ." Young Emily seized her hand.

"I don't know who they are, Blinda, they just appeared. And then this person who says she's me barged into my head, and I want her OUT!" The girl grimaced and Aunt Emily said, "Blinda, thank heavens! We're in quite a pickle. We need your help; you must do something." Blinda stood up and took Emily by the shoulders, peering into her eyes.

"Good heavens," she gasped. "A Doubler! Two of you, old and young, in the same body. I've heard of it but I've never seen one. It won't do, you know, it won't do at all. But here, come sit down, all of you, and tell me about it." They sat around the table to tell their story. Every so often Young Emily would interrupt, which seemed to infuriate Aunt Emily.

"I must ask you to be silent until we have finished speaking!" Aunt Emily said.

"But I want to know what it's like in your time! Is everyone allowed to wear such nice comfortable clothing? And what about all this Magnet magic? And who is—OW!" A smug look crossed Young Emily's face.

"*That* should keep her quiet," said Aunt Emily.

"Emily! What have you done?" cried Blinda.

"I pinched her. Hard."

Falcon stared at her aunt, who ignored Blinda's protests and continued her account of their travel through time. She had never seen Aunt Emily behave like this before. There was a triumphant look in her eyes that was almost frightening.

"So then we landed, and here I am, young and strong and healthy again." Emily stretched her arms over her head and smiled.

"You can't stay here," said the witch. "You must know that." Aunt Emily nodded.

"Oh, I know; you're quite right, of course. That's why I . . . *we've* come to you for help. We need to get back to the time before I had the attack, so it can be prevented."

Blinda rubbed her nose with her forefinger, which always helped her think. "It's a tall order, and time travel is not my forte. You say you've done it before, Allie? With Mr. Quigley?"

"Well, not just with him, with my brother and our friend, but Mr. Quigley has done it several times, and he *was* a shaman. Or, that is, he will be." Allie squinted with the effort of trying to make sense of Time.

"Then I think we'd best go see him right away. You know him, don't you, Emily? Didn't he teach that watercolor class you took last year? Is he on the telephone, do you know?"

"I don't know," said Young Emily in a sulky voice, "I don't know anything, do I? I'm just a child."

"Don't pout, Emily, it's most unbecoming. Come along then; we'll just have to chance it. Thank goodness your parents are in London for the season." Blinda started out of the room and then stopped, looking at Falcon and Allie.

"But first we'd better get you some proper clothing or we'll be arrested. Falcon, you can wear something of Emily's, and Allie, I think my things will fit you, lengthwise at least."

Soon Falcon and Allie were dressed in clothes of the period, more or less. Falcon wore a dress very like Emily's that fit quite well, but Allie, in one of Blinda's skirts and a blouse, looked very odd. Blinda was much fatter than Allie, so the belt around her waist had to be pulled tight to keep her skirt up, and the blouse was several sizes too big. The clothes were heavy and uncomfortable, even with their own underwear underneath, and they had to wear their own sandals as their feet were much bigger than Emily's or Blinda's. The witch looked at them and shook her head.

"Well, it's the best I can do on short notice," she said. "We'll just have to brazen it out in front of the servants." She put a small basket over her arm and led them downstairs. The butler opened the door for them, bowing stiffly at the waist.

"We're going out, Graves," said Blinda. "We shall be home for dinner."

"Shall I fetch the carriage, Miss Cholmondely?"

"No thank you, Graves. We'll take a cab."

"Allow me, Miss Cholmondely," said the butler, and he hailed a hansom cab on 21st Street. They climbed in and started uptown toward Central Park and the museum.

# CHAPTER SIX

I T TOOK THEM WELL OVER AN HOUR TO GET TO THE museum. Falcon and Allie were surprised by how crowded the streets were. There were various sorts of carriages and delivery wagons, and once a high, rickety-looking car that made a lot of noise and scared the horses. It was a cool, breezy day, but the smell of horse manure, smoke, and sewage nearly choked them until they drew near the park. They got out of the hansom cab opposite the huge red stone pile of the American Museum of Natural History.

Falcon and Allie really did look quite peculiar, and they left a wake of astonishment and disapproval behind them as they walked up the steps.

Inside, the rotunda was a very different place from the airy, well-lit space they were used to. The light was dim, and instead of the soaring drama of the barosaurus group that Falcon was used to, glass-topped wooden cases lined the walls, holding an assortment of birds, animal skins, and dried plants, all looking faded, forlorn, and extremely dead.

The people walking from case to case were dwarfed by the high ceiling, the low murmur of their voices swallowed up by the immensity of the hall. Fortunately most of them were too absorbed by the wonders of the museum to notice the oddly dressed girls. A guard, however, did. He hurried over to intercept them as they approached the information desk.

"Just a minute, you gypsies, you can't come in here dressed like that. Just you run along outside!" He loomed over them in a threatening manner, his enormous black mustache bristling with authority.

"It's quite all right, officer," said Blinda as Falcon and Allie cringed under the gaze of the people who had turned to see what the commotion was.

"They're with me, Mr. Hawkins," Blinda continued. "They are going to pose for Mr. Quigley, for the background of a new diorama he's painting. These are their costumes."

The guard's face cleared, and he beamed at them.

"Why, it's Miss Cholmondely and Miss Emily, isn't it? I do beg pardon, young ladies. Friends of Mr. Quigley's—I had no idea. A grand fellow he is, and a fine artist to be sure. Now what would you be dressed up as, if I might inquire, meaning no disrespect but only ignorant as I am of these here exotic places?"

"Tasmania," said Allie, without missing a beat. "Mr. Quigley is painting a scene of Tasmanian devils with . . . boogaloos in the foreground."

"Tastefully stuffed and mounted by Mr. Akeley himself," said Blinda.

"Yes, in realistic postures, and with us dressed as Tasmanian natives doing one of their hunting dances," said Falcon.

"Well, I'll be jiggered!" said the guard. "Boogaloos, you say. I've always wanted to see one of them. Fierce they are, so I've heard."

"Very," said Aunt Emily. "Man-eaters."

"You don't say," said the guard. "Well, I'd take you up to Mr. Quigley myself, I would, only I can't leave my post, you see. But you know where his workshop is, Miss Emily. You go straight in. He might not hear you knock when he's working— he's that artistic, you see. He don't allow for aught but painting when he's painting."

They thanked the helpful guard, who returned to his post, murmuring, "Tasmania! One of them South American places, I expect. Terrible things, man-eaters."

The four walked through the enormous museum, and after quite a long time they came to a door labeled WORKSHOP #3. Blinda knocked, just to be polite, but when nobody answered she seized the doorknob and they walked in.

They found themselves in a large room flooded with light from the long windows that lined one wall. It smelled strongly of paint. Huge panels of canvas were tacked along another wall, two of them tinted in graduated shades of pale blue, darker at the top. A tall, stout man in a paint-smeared smock stood with his back to them, hands clasped behind him, as he gazed into the expanse of painted sky.

"Storm," he said to himself. "Yes, that's it. A lowering storm, greenish light, and the herd fleeing before it in a great sweep of—" He flung his arm out in a dramatic gesture, knocking over a jar full of brushes that stood on a nearby table.

"Great jumping Jehoshaphat!" he said, lunging for the brushes. He halted in mid-lunge when he saw his visitors.

"Who?" he said. He stared at Falcon and Allie for a minute, looking puzzled, but he brightened when he recognized Emily.

"Emily Davies! What a splendid surprise! Is this your mother?" An anxious expression crossed his face as he brushed at his smock, adding a smear of sky blue to its multicolored surface. He ran a hand through his untidy hair to no effect.

"No, Mr. Quigley, this is my governess, Blinda Cholmondely. And these are my . . . my friends. This is Falcon and this is Allie."

Quigley shook hands with each of them, looking immensely pleased. To Allie, who had met him before in another time and place, he looked just as she remembered, though he was dressed differently and was considerably fatter and cleaner in spite of the paint. He didn't seem to notice their clothing at all, unlike everyone else they had encountered so far.

"Luncheon!" said Mr. Quigley happily, wiping his hands on a rag and removing his smock. Underneath it he wore high-waisted black trousers and a collarless white shirt with the sleeves rolled up. He rolled them down and began struggling to attach a stiffly starched collar to the neckband. It seemed to give him a great deal of trouble.

"Allow me, Mr. Quigley," said Blinda.

"If you would be so kind, Miss Cholmondely," said Quigley.

54

"I'm all thumbs with these plaguey things." Blinda tamed the collar and tied the red and blue necktie that Quigley handed her.

"There!" said the witch, giving the tie a pat. "All shipshape and Bristol fashion, Mr. Quigley."

"Thank you, Miss Cholmondely, I *am* grateful." Quigley put on a long black coat and beamed at them.

"We'll go to Louis Sherry's," he said. "I have an account there. Superb shad this time of year—black butter and capers, you know. Delicious. You liked the sweetbreads sous cloche as I recall, dear Emily, and for Miss Cholmondely and your friends here—"

"Mr. Quigley," said Blinda, "I don't think we'd better go out. You look simply splendid, but Falcon and Allie are not dressed properly at all, and people stare so. We've come to ask for your help, you see. We're in a bit of trouble."

"Trouble!" said Quigley, looking apprehensive. "Good heavens, how dreadful! Oh dear, not money trouble, I hope. Not much good at that, you know."

"Oh no, Mr. Quigley," said Falcon, who was beginning to like this stout and peculiar man. "It's only that Aunt Emily got so sick and Allie had done the spinning through time before with you, you know, so we did it too, and here we are, and she's all well now—Emily that is—but only twelve years old, and we need to get back."

Quigley's eyes seemed about to bulge right out of their sockets, and he pulled nervously at the knot in his tie. He edged over to Emily, never taking his eyes off Falcon, and whispered behind his hand, "Lunatic, is she? Lost her mind, poor child— is that it? Or brain fever? And this one too . . . a dreadful thing in such young ladies." He pressed his hand against Allie's forehead.

"No fever as yet," he said. "My poor Emily, how can I help you?"

Emily giggled, and there was a visible struggle in her face between the twelve-year-old Emily who thought Mr. Quigley's reaction was terribly funny, and the hundred-and-thirteen-year-old Emily who knew they were in a great deal of trouble. For the moment, the old Emily won.

"Nobody's crazy, Mr. Quigley," she said. "If you would just hear me out, I'll tell you all about it."

"Nothing easier, dear child. Here, have a seat, all of you young ladies." He moved tubes of paint, brushes, rags, coffee cups, and a box of animal crackers off a battered sofa and cleared a couple of chairs of sketchbooks and boxes labeled PHOTOGRAPHS: AFRICAN VELDT 1901. They sat down, and Emily began to tell the story of what had happened in New York City more than a hundred years in the future. (Or what *would* happen, depending on how you look at it. Verb tenses are quite useless in these situations.)

# CHAPTER SEVEN

"AND," SAID EMILY, SITTING BACK AND FOLDING her hands in her lap, "that's the gist of it, I think. Oh, and you have met Allie before, of course."

"What?" said Quigley, who was already thoroughly confused by Emily's tale.

"Yes sir, Mr. Quigley," said Allie, "only you wouldn't remember it because it hasn't happened yet. Well, I mean, it has in a way, because it was thirty thousand years ago, but for you it won't happen till 1913."

Hieronymous Quigley thrust his hands into his already tousled mop of hair.

"Oh dear, oh dear. I don't know, I really don't—it's all a dreadful muddle, isn't it? My head is simply spinning."

"It's all right, Mr. Quigley," said Falcon, who thought Allie and Emily had made the whole thing far too complicated. "It's only that we need to get back to our own time."

"And she has to get out of my head," said Young Emily, who had kept quiet till now. Quigley jumped and stared at the girl.

"Emily?" he said. "Are you quite well?"

"I'm perfectly well, Mr. Quigley, only I've got my old self in my head with me and I want her out. I'm sure you and Blinda can help. She's my governess but what she *really* is, is a witch."

"Oh no, Emily, I'm sure you're wrong. Miss Cholmondely is a charming person—anyone can see that."

"Not that sort of witch—a good witch. She can do magic," said Young Emily.

"But we have to be careful," said Allie, "not to change anything in this time, or we might not be able to get back." She wished Fig were here to explain better. He was so good at science. She tried to remember exactly what he had said about Time.

"It's like a carousel," she said. "A merry-go-round." It sounded really lame, and nobody seemed to find her explanation very helpful. A new thought struck her, and she turned to Emily.

"And, Ms. Davies, I don't know how to get you back before your heart attack. Fig and I got home eighteen hours after we'd left, even though we'd been in the past for weeks and weeks. We couldn't control it at all."

"I'm sure there's a way," said Blinda. "I'll just have to find out what it is."

While Blinda went through her basket, searching for the right spell, Mr. Quigley made an effort to tidy up his studio. After a few minutes of watching him move one pile from table to chair to sofa and back, the three girls pitched in to help. Falcon noticed that Quigley seemed to be in the habit of spending the night in the studio. There was a toothbrush in a glass by the sink, some clothes in a cupboard, and a primitive-looking hotplate on a table in the corner.

Blinda looked up from her basket. "None of these spells will do, I'm afraid. I have many more at home, in my house in the village. In the meantime we'll just have to put our heads together. Dear me. Well, can't think on an empty stomach, I always say. I've brought us a nice luncheon." She set the basket on a low table near the windows.

Hieronymous Quigley looked pleased for a moment, but his face fell when he realized that the basket was far too small to hold enough for five.

"How kind of you, Miss Cholmondely. I'm sure these young ladies will appreciate it. I couldn't eat a thing myself— had an enormous breakfast, you know: bacon, eggs, sausage, mushrooms. Flapjacks," he said heroically as Blinda opened the basket and pulled out a blue and white checked tablecloth. She smiled at him.

"I do hope you'll be able to nibble at something, Mr. Quigley. I've brought plenty for all of us."

And out of the small wicker basket came five sets of willowware dishes, five crystal tumblers, five sets of flatware, five blue linen napkins, *and* a handsome tureen of consommé with Madeira. There were five grilled trout, shoestring potatoes, a bowl of new peas with lettuce, a basket of hot rolls, a tub of sweet butter stamped with a broomstick, and a wooden tray of cheeses (Port Salut, Stilton, Gruyère, and Cheshire).

Falcon and Emily struggled not to laugh at Allie's and Mr. Quigley's faces as Blinda took more and more food out of the tiny basket, covering all but the very edges of the checkered cloth and filling the room with the most delicious smells. Allie's eyes grew bigger and bigger as each dish appeared, while Mr. Quigley loosened his tie and began to mop his face with a large handkerchief, murmuring, "Good heavens! Well, I never! Hot rolls—it's a miracle!" At that, Emily gave an unladylike snort and burst out laughing.

"Oh dear, oh dear, Mr. Quigley, your face . . . oh my!"

Blinda looked as severe as her cheerful face would allow.

"Emily Alexandra Davies, I'll thank you to pull yourself together and behave properly or there will be no luncheon for you at all, young lady. Now then, Mr. Quigley, do you think you might manage just a little of the soup?"

"Perhaps just a spoonful, if you please, Miss Cholmondely," said Quigley as Blinda ladled out a generous portion.

They toasted Blinda with sparkling Spanish cider and set to. Everything was delicious, piping hot where it should be hot, cold where it should be cold. Mr. Quigley's face grew shiny with happiness and butter, and Allie realized, as she had not before, just how difficult it would be for him to live in the Ice Age without hot rolls or Stilton.

"Oh, I almost forgot, I brought a special treat," said Blinda, reaching into the inexhaustible basket.

"I remembered, Emily, you said Mr. Quigley was particularly fond of huckleberries. I put these up last summer." She pulled out a beautifully latticed pie filled with tiny purple berries and a jug of thick yellow cream to go with it.

Emily's eyes lit up with glee.

"H-U-uckle-uckle, B-U-buckle-buckle, that spells huckle-berry pie! H-U-uckle-uckle, B-U-buckle-buckle, that spells huckleberry PIE!" she sang.

Blinda and Mr. Quigley looked astonished, but they applauded enthusiastically when the song was over.

"That's most amusing, Emily," said Blinda, smiling, "and a great compliment to my pie. Where on earth did you learn such a song?" She was giving Mr. Quigley a particularly large slice.

"Oh," said Aunt Emily, "I heard it in a vaudeville show at Tony Pastor's, when I was a kid. A funny little fat man who called himself the 'King of Unadilla '"

"Why, I've seen him," said Quigley, cutting through the flaky crust into the dark, juicy filling. "A luscious pie, Miss Cholmondely, I do thank you. But I never heard him sing anything like that. He has a fine voice, but the only song he seems to know is 'Believe Me if All Those Endearing Young Charms.' Awfully tiresome after the first few times. He's usually first on the bill."

"But isn't that good?" asked Falcon.

"Oh no," said Quigley. "Worst spot on the bill. People are still coming in, you see. Talking, moving about. It's a fine place, though, Tony Pastor's is. Wonderful performers—well, except for that poor Unadilla fellow. Perhaps, Miss Cholmondely, you and Miss Emily and these young ladies would do me the honor of accompanying me to Pastor's to see the show. There's a remarkable magician called Mr. Miracle, and a dog act . . ."

"Dear me, Mr. Quigley," said Blinda. "I hardly think Emily's mother would approve of her seeing a vaudeville show."

"Oh, it's all good clean fun at Pastor's, Miss Cholmondely.

Nothing at all improper, I do assure you. I would never suggest such a thing," said Quigley, blushing.

"Yes, let's go! I always loved vaudeville," said Aunt Emily.

"Oh please, let's do. Mama would hate it, but she's in London and I've never been to a vaudeville. Do let's go, Blinda," Young Emily begged.

"Well, then—" began Blinda, but Falcon interrupted her.

"Blinda, we can't waste time going to shows. We have to figure out how to go back to our time."

"Oh drat, I suppose we do." The witch stuffed everything back into the basket and snapped her fingers.

"Tea!" she said. A golf tee appeared in her hand.

"No no no! T-E-A, I said! Lapsang souchong, very strong. I need to think." A steaming mug bearing the words SOUVENIR OF WALLA WALLA appeared in her hand. She began to pace, sipping as she talked and nearly baptizing everyone with scalding tea.

"Time travel," said the witch. "Extremely complicated . . . one is always doubling back on oneself . . . very dangerous. Changing the past. Risky. And one never knows—you might go out like blown candles: *POOF!* Let's see . . ."

Blinda's first suggestion was that the girls try spinning as they had before.

"But if it works, Aunt Emily will be dying again. Couldn't we go back to before she got sick and take her to the hospital to prevent it?" Falcon was sure Blinda could do it if she would only try.

"I have to go," said Emily.

"I know, dear, we're working on it," said Blinda.

"No, I mean to the ladies' room," said Emily. "Where is it, Mr. Quigley?"

Mr. Quigley became terribly flustered at being asked so intimate a question, but he managed to mumble, "Er, down the corridor to the left and round the corner there's the . . . um, the whatsit . . . I mean, the . . ."

"Toilet," said Emily in a loud voice.

Blinda and Falcon went down the hall with Emily, who snickered all the way at the look on Mr. Quigley's face. Falcon thought that either the twelve-year-old Emily was taking over, or else her hundred-and-thirteen-year-old aunt had a lot of Young Emily still in her.

"The latter, I think," said Blinda, reading Falcon's mind in the disconcerting way she had. "Emily, you should be ashamed of yourself, embarrassing that nice man."

"You forget, Blinda, that I am not a child but entirely your equal. There's no need to speak to me in that admonitory tone." Emily stalked ahead of them and let the door of the ladies' washroom slam in their faces.

When they entered, they saw Emily's feet under the door of the stall and heard her voice singing, "Passengers will please refrain from flushing toilets while the train is standing in the station; I love you . . ."

"What a dreadful song," said Blinda. Emily sang louder. When Falcon and Blinda were ready to leave, Blinda said, "I'm sorry, Emily. It's hard to remember there are two of you and that one of you is an adult. I do beg your pardon."

"Granted," said Aunt Emily, stepping out of the stall. "Oh

drat! I always hated these things." One of her black stockings had fallen down around her ankles.

"I hate them too," said Young Emily.

Blinda pulled a handful of safety pins from her pocket. "I'll pin them to your drawers, dear." She knelt and pinned the stockings to the long cotton pants under Emily's dress.

"Blinda," said Falcon, "maybe if we spin in a hospital, we'd still be there when we got back. Then the doctors could keep Emily from getting sick. Is Mount Sinai here in this time?" The witch closed the last safety pin and stood up.

"There," she said. "That's better. I must say, your twenty-first-century underwear is a great improvement on what we have nowadays! Falcon, I don't know enough about this time travel business yet. I don't know how much it can be controlled. You'll just have to wait until I've done some research."

# CHAPTER EIGHT

Back in the workshop, Allie was trying to explain to Quigley about going into the Ice Age. She was having a good deal of trouble getting him to understand that he would go too, in about ten years, and that they would meet there.

"But we've already met!" said Quigley. "Why would—" Just then Falcon, Blinda, and Emily walked in.

"Mr. Quigley," said the witch, "we must go to my house in the village. Most of my spells are there, and I'm sure there's something about time travel. Come along, girls."

Quigley led them to a small half-hidden doorway on the 81st Street side of the building to avoid running into the nosy guard. He hailed a passing hansom cab.

"I've been no help at all," he said sadly. "Really, I feel quite useless." His normally jolly face looked as droopy as a basset hound's.

Allie patted his arm.

"It's okay, Mr. Quigley. Time travel is really complicated."

"Indeed it is," said Blinda. "And I hope you will take us to Tony Pastor's sometime soon, once we've got this all settled. You've been most kind."

"Oh, yes indeed," said Quigley. "I would be honored, delighted."

They piled into the waiting cab and Blinda instructed the driver, "Charles Street and Washington, please." Mr. Quigley stood on the curb, waving as they drove off.

The three girls sat quietly as the cab took them downtown. Allie was trying to figure out the complications of Time, wishing she had paid more attention to her brother.

Falcon nibbled on a thumbnail and tried to remember why she had cared so much about Lily Weng. She didn't seem to matter at all now. *She won't even be born for ninety years; her great-grandparents are probably still in China,* she thought.

They passed a man selling something like snow cones from a cart.

"Oh, do let's stop!" cried Aunt Emily. "I'd love a lemon hokey-pokey. It's been years, and I'm so thirsty." But Blinda was busy writing in a small pocket notebook and paid no attention.

They were passing through Hell's Kitchen, where thousands of poor Irish immigrants lived in crowded tenements along 9th Avenue. The smell was awful, and Falcon wondered aloud how people could live like this.

"They have no choice," said Blinda. "They are terribly poor, and the city does little to help them."

"It's not right!" said Allie.

"No, it's not," said Young Emily. "I shall speak to my papa, when he returns from London."

"You'll be wasting your breath," said Aunt Emily. "Papa owns several of those tenements and makes a tidy profit from them. He'll tell you the Irish are just animals and don't deserve any better."

"That's a lie! You, you get out of my head this minute!" Young Emily burst into tears. Falcon put her arm around the sobbing girl. She thought her great-great-aunt was being very mean to her younger self.

"Where exactly are we going, Miss Cholmondely?" Allie asked.

"To my house on Charles Street. You'll be safe there while we figure out how to get you back without letting Emily die," said the witch.

"But you're living at my parents' house with me," said Young Emily.

"Oh yes, but with your parents away in London, we'll have more freedom. Falcon and Allie can stay at my house, and we'll come by every day." The cab pulled up on Charles Street before a high stone wall festooned with lilacs. A tall sour cherry tree behind the wall hung its pink blossoms over their heads.

It was just as Falcon remembered it from a year ago. *Well, actually, not a year ago, a hundred years in the future,* she thought. *A year ago for me.* She began to understand why Allie's story about time travel was so confusing.

Blinda led them through a gate in the wall, half hidden by ivy. There stood the small green and white cottage. It was surrounded by a smooth lawn that was dotted with dandelions and crocuses, bordered with brimming beds of daffodils and jonquils. There was a green and white doghouse in one corner with a sign over the entrance that read BEWARE OF THE CALOPUS.

Just as they reached the cottage, they heard a screech and the door flew open with a crash. An enormous cat streaked through the doorway, his orange fur puffed out so he was twice his normal size. He raced up the cherry tree to crouch on a limb, his green eyes blazing.

"I won't have it!" hissed the cat. "I simply will not have it!" He began grooming himself while Allie stared. She had never seen a talking cat before.

"Augustus!" exclaimed Falcon in delight. Blinda sighed.

"I'm sorry, Augustus. I'll speak to him again," she said to the cat.

"Humph!" said the cat, raising his hind leg straight up and washing behind it in a haughty manner.

The group entered the cottage.

"It wasn't my fault," said a plaintive voice as a plateful of cookies materialized in the air and set itself down on the coffee table in the living room. "I was baking and he got underfoot. I didn't mean to step on his tail." A tray holding a jug and five glasses plonked onto the table beside the cookies, splashing onto a copy of *Every Witchway, the Sorcerer's Quarterly.* Blinda mopped at the mess with her handkerchief.

"This is Humphrey," she said, waving a hand in the air. "He's my caretaker while I live at your house, Emily. Say hello, Humphrey."

A Bronx cheer exploded wetly beside Allie's left ear.

"Hello, Humphrey," said a mocking voice that then cackled with laughter. The laughter was followed by the unmistakable sound of a loud fart.

"Humphrey!" said Blinda. "Leave the room at once." The door slammed, leaving a strong smell of chocolate floating in the air. Blinda motioned to the girls to sit down and poured them all lemonade from the jug. Emily, whose mouth was very dry, took a big gulp and wished she hadn't. The lemonade was extremely sour and tasted of fish.

Blinda tasted her own glassful, made a face, and set it down.

"He's made it with clam juice and no sugar again. I'm sorry. Boggarts don't make very good cooks, I'm afraid." This certainly seemed to be true. The cookies were burnt black and as hard as coal.

After several tries, producing in succession a large bottle of gin, a small replica of the Trevi fountain in pink plastic, and a mechanical tin mermaid that played "How Dry I Am" when you twisted her tail, the witch managed to supply them all with large mugs of apple juice, which they drank gratefully after the dusty cab ride.

"Why did his fart smell like chocolate?" asked Allie, who could still detect its presence in the air.

"He thinks chocolate is the worst smell in the world. He *is* extremely rude. Boggarts always are, but Humphrey will protect you fiercely from anyone who tries to harm you or enter my garden. And he's really quite good at housework. Perhaps you girls could manage the cooking while you're here?"

"We'll have to," said Falcon. "Or we'll starve."

Aunt Emily was reluctant to leave Allie and Falcon on their own with the unreliable boggart, but Blinda assured her that the girls would be fine as long as they didn't go outside the stone wall.

"Don't leave the grounds without me," she said. "There's no telling what might happen if you were to go out. Even the smallest thing—buying a hot dog, petting a kitten, tripping on a curbstone—might change the future in some terrible way. It might even change things so that you two would never be born at all, and then you'd become—" Blinda stopped abruptly, and her usually rosy face turned pale. "Well, never mind that now. Just stay here inside the garden wall. Humphrey will get you anything you want, and I'll come by every day with Emily to do research in my magic file. Together we'll figure out a way to get you all back to your own time."

"Without me dying," said Aunt Emily.

"And get her out of my head," said Young Emily.

"Precisely," said Blinda, leading Emily outside and through the gate.

Falcon and Allie watched them through the iron bars of the gate until they disappeared round the corner. Falcon sighed as she turned back to the house.

"What's the matter, Falcon?" asked Allie, who was interested to see that the house was now purple and white and that the sign over the matching doghouse read BEWARE OF THE BARQUEST.

"Magic is always so . . . messy." Falcon thought of the pleasant dullness of the day as it should have been: a visit with Aunt

Emily, a chat with Ana, a swim in the afternoon, and dinner with Freddy Maldonado. It seemed a thousand years ago.

"Chicken chilequiles," she murmured to herself.

"What?"

"Freddy Maldonado, he's our friend who works at the museum. He sends out for Mexican from Carlita's and my favorite is chicken chilequiles. It's tortillas with—"

"I know!" said Allie. "I know Dr. Maldonado too. He came for Christmas with us last year. We order from Carlita's all the time when we're living with my aunt Bijou. She has to pay a delivery fee because it's too far from Sutton Place, but it's worth it. Did you ever have their—"

"Foreign muck!" said a voice, as an enormous mole appeared on the lawn. The mole's voice was familiar.

"Humphrey?" said Falcon.

"Aye, though by rights it should be Mister Boggart to you, young miss. No manners, children these days."

In spite of his words the boggart's tone was quite friendly as he squatted in a corner of the garden and began to turn over the earth with his paws.

"Can we help you, Hum . . . Mr. Boggart?" asked Allie, watching the creature pick a long red earthworm from the dark soil and place it in a silver bowl.

"Nay, thank ye kindly all the same. A dozen of these should do us nicely for supper." A wave of nausea washed over Allie and she gulped.

"Supper?" she said. The boggart stood up and walked toward the cottage, holding the bowl, which now contained a writhing knot of worms. As he approached the house he dematerialized, and the last they saw was the bowl of worms bobbing two feet above the ground as the purple door opened. Allie turned to Falcon.

"I can't eat worms! I'll throw up. What'll we do? Do you think we could send out for pizza?"

"I'm pretty sure they didn't have pizza delivery in 1903," said Falcon, trying to remember Aunt Emily's stories about her childhood. "But I can cook. I mean, I can cook some things, like omelets."

"Oh then, please, Falcon—quick! Let's stop Humphrey before he makes something disgusting and we have to eat it to be polite." Allie had eaten some very yucky things in the Ice Age, and she was not eager to do it again.

*I wouldn't eat earthworms, no matter what,* Falcon thought to herself. Allie was kind of prissy to worry about being rude to a mole or a boggart or whatever Humphrey was supposed to be. But Falcon liked to cook, and Blinda's house had a small but delightful kitchen that looked out on the garden. Herbs and vegetables grew in a plot by the side door. She followed Allie into the house.

To their relief, Humphrey Boggart was perfectly happy to let Falcon do the cooking and wasn't at all offended by the offer.

"To tell the truth, dearios, I'm run off my feet just doing the housework and gardening. Especially with that doghouse. Today it's a calopus or a barquest, but yesterday it was a basilisk and the lawn was simply littered with dead birds. Then Wednesday it was a wyvern, and such a mess as you would not believe . . . I'll have to put in a new bed of irises—and that with my back not being at all what it should be. Now then, let me show you where everything is, and then I'll go put my feet up and be glad of it, I can tell you! What do you fancy cooking?"

"Well," said Falcon, "omelets, maybe, and a salad, and, er . . . muffins? Do you have any eggs?"

"Yes indeed," said Humphrey, opening the door of the old-fashioned icebox. "Duck, griffin, Harpy, or hen?"

"Um, hen, I guess," said Falcon, looking at the griffin's egg, which was the size of a bowling ball and had a sinister green glow.

Humphrey Boggart showed her where everything was. She secretly resolved to get rid of the boogers, gravel, belly-button lint, and toenail clippings that were stored in neatly labeled glass jars in the cupboards.

"Don't use up all the gravel, deary, if you don't mind. We're running a bit low," said the boggart, who had materialized as a giant frog. He settled himself on the sofa in the living room and disappeared slowly, starting with his webbed green feet.

Falcon caught Allie's eye and Allie looked back with a face full of laughter. *This might not be so bad,* thought Falcon. *She could turn out to be a real friend.*

Allie picked a crisp head of romaine from the garden and cut some sprigs of chervil and thyme. She had learned a little about simple cooking from her aunt Bijou, so she acted as Falcon's helper, washing lettuce, crushing garlic for salad dressing, grating cheese for the omelets. Falcon had never made a whole meal by herself before, and it was tricky getting everything to come out at the same time. The omelets were done before the muffins so they had to eat them cold, and the oven's heat was uneven so two of the muffins got a little scorched.

But everything tasted fine. Humphrey Boggart ate the burnt muffins with great enthusiasm, spreading them with a thick layer of vaseline and dead flies.

"You'll make a grand cook, deary," he said.

"Thank you, Mr. Boggart," said Falcon, keeping a straight face with great difficulty.

"Oh, call me Humphrey, my dears, since we're going to be here together all snug, as you might say. No, no, I won't hear of you washing up, that's my job. You stick to cooking, I'll do the rest. Take a turn in the garden, why don't you? It's perfectly safe with that barquest. Don't let the howling bother you."

The girls were a bit nervous, never having seen or heard of a barquest, but they went outside. It was dusk, and the smell of lilacs floated on the cool spring air. No sound came from the doghouse, which was barely visible in its shadowy corner. A light breeze blew through the branches of the cherry tree, and a shower of blossoms, like pink snowflakes, fluttered to the grass.

They sat in two of the Adirondack chairs that stood around a low table on the lawn.

"It's so quiet," said Allie. It was. They heard the wind in the trees and the sound of a wagon or carriage passing by, the *clip-clop* of the horse's hooves, the jingle of the harness. Nearby, someone was playing a mandolin and singing in a language they did not recognize. A man spoke, a woman laughed in response. On the river, not far away, a boat horn blew; it was a lost and lonely sound. The voice of a city, a large and bustling city, on an April evening in 1903. But there were no cars or trucks, no planes overhead, no amplified music. Strangest of all was the absence of that low incessant roar that was the pulse of New York City in the twenty-first century, the breathing of a great beast that never sleeps.

"I like it here," said Falcon.

"You mean this time, 1903?" asked Allie. Falcon shook her head.

"No, not that exactly. I want to go back even if Aunt Emily doesn't . . ." She turned her mind away from the thought and curled her legs under her. The evening was growing chilly.

"I mean this garden," Falcon said. "It's a good place. Like the museum is, and some places in the park."

Allie nodded. "Yes! I know. And the ocean, only not in summer, when it's crowded, but in winter, when it's empty and you can hear the waves crashing. All those places, they all . . ." She paused, thinking, hugging her knees to her chest. A whippoorwill called as the darkness gathered around them.

Falcon shivered.

"This Magnet thing," she said. "What do you suppose it means?"

Allie did not reply for a minute or two.

"I don't know," she said at last. "Emily said it meant protecting the Magic. Maybe it's being a part of those good places, caring for them. That's what they are, I think, the museum and here and the others."

"Magic," said Falcon.

"Yes. Magic."

*Maybe that would be okay,* thought Falcon. *Maybe being a Magnet won't be so bad. . . .*

"Do you think Blinda can get us home?" asked Allie.

"I think so. I mean, I don't know for sure, but she's really a pretty good witch, even if she seems kind of wacky some-times. I'm not so worried about that as about my aunt Emily. I guess she can't stay here, but I don't want her to die."

Allie was quiet for a long time, scrunched down in the chair with her long legs stretched out in front of her. Her skirt had hiked up so Falcon could see her knobby knees.

"How old did you say she was?"

"Aunt Emily? A hundred and . . . just over a hundred, I think." Falcon squirmed in her chair, wishing she had never brought up the subject of her great-great-aunt.

"It's 1903, and Young Emily said she was twelve." Allie stared into space, calculating. "That means she was born in 1891. So in our time she's a hundred and thirteen. That's really *old*, Falcon."

Falcon tried to see Allie's face through the dusk. "So? Lots of people get to be really old. That guy on television, Willard something? He's always saying happy birthday to people over a hundred. There are jillions of them!"

Allie didn't answer. They sat in the garden while the moon rose and the stars came out. After a while they went inside, up-stairs to the bedroom Blinda had made ready for them, where they soon fell asleep, breathing the scent of lilacs through the open window.

Uptown in Gramercy Park, Blinda and Emily were getting ready for bed. They had had a rather uncomfortable dinner under the eyes of Graves the butler and Polly the maid, who served the meal in the smaller of the two dining rooms. Blinda and Emily sat at one end of a table that seated twelve, trying to make polite conversation while one course followed another on large silver serving dishes that held enough for half a dozen hungry people.

Aunt Emily was used to having nothing more than milk and fruit in the evening. But Young Emily had only recently been promoted from nursery supper to dinner at eight with the grownups. She sat up straight like a lady, her spine never touching the back of the chair, and smiled happily as the parade of food began. Cream of celery soup, flounder hollandaise, lamb chops with watercress. When Graves approached her with the platter of chops there was a brief tussle. Aunt Emily said, "No thank you, Graves," just as Young Emily reached for the serving fork and spoon. Young Emily won, and with a splatter of gravy, a lamb chop flew onto her plate. Graves said nothing, and his face remained absolutely blank as the battle was repeated with a bowl of new potatoes. Polly's eyes were popping out of her head as she pushed through the leather-padded door into the kitchen, where Mrs. Hodge, the cook, sat with a cup of tea, resting her tired feet. Polly set the serving dishes down with a *THUNK* onto the long kitchen table.

"There's somethink funny about that child, make no mistake!" she said.

"You hold your tongue, Polly, and don't be speaking of yer betters so disrespectful. Wipe up that butter where you spilled it, and mind what yer doin'," said Mrs. Hodge.

In the dining room Young Emily's strong white teeth were chewing furiously on a bite of lamb chop. "I'll have indigestion, I'm quite certain," said Aunt Emily with her mouth full. "All this rich food just before bedtime—it's unwholesome."

"It's not! It's very good, and I'm hungry!"

"You can't possibly be hungry after all that fish."

"Well, I am. It's *my* body, you know, and I'm still growing."

All this was said in a low, hissing whisper, but anyone could see that Miss Emily seemed to be having a terrible argument with herself. Blinda watched Graves struggling to maintain his impassive expression. She spoke to Emily under her breath.

"Emily! Stop this at once. We can discuss your . . . predicament when we are alone. In the meantime, if you cannot speak in a civilized manner, do not speak at all."

"Graves," she said in a louder voice, "Miss Emily is overtired. Please have Molly bring a glass of milk to the nursery. We will not have any salad or dessert tonight." The butler bowed and went into the kitchen.

"I want my dessert!" Emily protested. "Mrs. Hodge has made lemon crème with brandied raspberries, and I'm *starving!*" She grabbed the last potato on her plate and crammed it into her mouth. Her face turned red as Aunt Emily refused to chew or swallow, until finally Blinda reached into Emily's mouth and pulled out the potato. Sparks seemed to shoot out of Blinda's brown eyes as she folded her napkin and stood up. She pointed toward the hall.

"Upstairs. This instant. And no more NONSENSE!"

# CHAPTER NINE

OVER THE NEXT WEEK, FALCON AND ALLIE SET-
tled into a routine. They got into the habit of getting
up very early to prevent Humphrey Boggart from helping them with
breakfast. As a result, Falcon was getting a chance to do a lot
more cooking than she did at home, where they ate take-out
food more often than not. When Missy did cook, the results
were, as Falcon told Allie, almost as bad as Humphrey's.

Allie grinned. "Boogers and gravel?" she said.

"Well, not exactly. But everything burnt or half raw and
the lettuce not washed."

Falcon and Allie had no time to get bored or restless.
Blinda came by every day as promised, with Emily in tow and
both Emilies squabbling all the way. They all found this tire-
some, and Blinda began to look rather harried. Even Humphrey
Boggart got sick of it and took to hiding when Blinda and
Emily appeared. He always showed up for lunch, though.

So did Mr. Quigley, several times. He brought everything he could find on time travel: H. G. Wells's *The Time Machine,* Jackson McCulloch's *A Journey to the Future,* and Mrs. Hawes's *Remembering Tomorrow.* He also told them about the wonderful shows he'd seen at Tony Pastor's.

"Sand dancers!" he said. "And that Mr. Miracle! Miracle indeed. I do believe he could do just about anything. There's no one like him and that's a fact—no, not even Harry Houdini himself. Is that rhubarb pie I smell?"

After lunch Blinda retired to her office (*escaped,* thought Falcon) to research magic spells, and the girls went outside. Blinda's garden had the curious and pleasing faculty of being exactly the size you wanted at any particular time. If they wanted a good long walk, it expanded into a vast area of winding paths that wandered through woods, hills, and meadows. If they just wanted to sit and drink lemonade or play dominoes, it contracted back to its normal size, a small lawn surrounded by flower beds, the cherry tree casting a cool shade, and the scent of lilacs wafting over everything in the breeze. It was also invisible to outsiders.

"And a good thing too," said Aunt Emily, "what with all the peculiar creatures that live in that doghouse." Today it was a hippogriff, grazing quietly on the spring grass.

Once Emily was away from the witch, she (or they) squabbled less and became more like two separate people even though both were contained in the body of one small, gray-eyed girl. To Falcon and Allie it almost felt as though they were just four friends weeding the garden, climbing the cherry tree, or sprawling on the grass, talking. Falcon had never had a group of friends before, and she liked it. Lily Weng and Penny Alden seemed a thousand years away instead of only a hundred, she remarked as they sat breathless after a race around the garden.

"Only!" Allie said.

"Oh, you know what I mean. I just don't care what they think of me anymore. I don't know why I ever did."

"I've never met a Chinese person," said Young Emily. "Well, not a girl, anyway. Mr. Hong does Papa's dress shirts, but he doesn't have any children. At least I don't think he does."

"Oh, Lily's not Chinese. She's American. Her grandfather—no, great-grandfather—came from China, I think."

"Lily used to be such a nice little girl," said Aunt Emily. "We all had such lovely parties with my doll's tea set, and Ana made those tiny tartlets, and you girls laughed so. I didn't realize she'd become so horrid."

Allie was twisting a long strand of red hair around one finger and trying to picture Lily, who, as Falcon said, did seem a thousand years away. Lily and Penny had never bothered her or paid any attention to her at all.

"I don't think she's horrid exactly," she said. "Those kids, the popular ones, they just don't care about other kids. They're not mean on purpose."

"Yes they are!" said Falcon. "They call names and giggle behind my . . . behind people's backs. That's on purpose."

"I'd like to slap them!" Young Emily said fiercely. "I'd slap 'em and punch 'em like this!" She pounded the air with her fists.

"So would I!" said Aunt Emily, and all of them exploded into laughter. Falcon brought out a basket of russets, picked in October and stored in Blinda's cellar. Falcon loved the cellar. It was dim and cool, and the scent of apples and drying herbs filled the air with spicy sweetness. Jars of Blinda's jellies and preserves glowed from shelves along the wall beside jars of honey labeled SAINT'S GOLD.

Allie bit into an apple.

"I'm going to be a famous actress when I grow up," she said dreamily, her mouth full. She swallowed. "And an artist too. And my brother will be a scientist, and we'll live in the country and grow apples like this. How about you, Emily?"

A garbled sound came out of the girl's mouth, and she scowled.

"She's asking ME," said Young Emily. "You're already grown up; you're an old lady."

"I'm not!" Emily's face shimmered as though it were going to change into something else. This always happened when the two Emilies disagreed, and it made Falcon slightly queasy. She looked away.

"I suppose I *am* an old woman," said Aunt Emily. "But that's not all I am—nobody's just their age. But *do* tell us, *dear* Emily, just what you think you're going to be."

The malice in her voice surprised Falcon. *Why would Aunt Emily be so nasty to herself? It doesn't make sense.*

"Well, I'm not going to be like Mama," said Young Emily. "Just getting married and changing my clothes six times a day and going to boring parties. I'm going to be a writer and travel all over the world and have adventures."

"Oh really?" retorted Aunt Emily. "And what makes you think you'll be allowed to do all that? They're sending you off to finishing school in Switzerland next year, and in four years you'll make your debut in London. Then you'll marry some rich, respectable son from a rich, respectable family and have one perfect child, EXACTLY like your mother. Only *you're* not all that perfect. So there!"

"Aunt Emily!" cried Falcon. "That's not true—that's not what you did at all! You did become a writer and you've been everywhere and not gotten married. You've done everything you wanted—you said so."

"You did?" asked Young Emily. "I mean, I did? Or I will? Really?"

Aunt Emily sniffed. *"Hmph!* Not if you're such a namby-pamby as you are. 'Papa says so. Papa would *never . . .'* You'll have to see them for what they are, and you'll have to fight for everything you want." Her face was flushed and tears stood in her eyes.

The silence that followed this outburst was beginning to grow uncomfortable when Humphrey emerged from the cottage with a silver tray. He had taken the form of a large armadillo and was crossing the lawn with some difficulty, balancing the tray on his tiny forepaws with his shell clattering behind him. There was something on the tray that quivered and smelled really putrid.

"Thought you young ladies might like a little snack," he said.

# CHAPTER TEN

It was midmorning on the eighth day, and Falcon and Allie were digging in the garden. The weather had turned sunny and warm after a rainy night, and everything smelled newly washed. They were putting a border of marigolds around the herb garden to keep the ants away and picking sprigs of tarragon, chervil, and parsley for Montpellier butter, a recipe Falcon had found in one of Blinda's cookbooks. They had asked Humphrey to pick up shallots, spinach, and watercress along with the salmon on his shopping list.

For these daily errands the shape-shifting boggart transformed himself into a stout middle-aged woman named Mrs. Cubbins and toddled off each morning with a basket over his arm. Humphrey was thoroughly enjoying this break from cooking, and he ate all of Falcon's experiments with great enthusiasm. As long as she didn't use chocolate, he loved everything, though he often added a sprinkle of toenail clippings or mulch to his own portion, first offering them to the girls from a silver saltcellar.

Falcon and Allie had become friends in the past week. They began to know each other's lives while they made breakfast together in the mornings or worked in the garden. They giggled over the old-fashioned clothes Blinda had provided and agreed that they would definitely keep wearing their own twenty-first-century underwear.

"How do they stand it?" wondered Allie aloud, folding the long, heavy linen underpants and camisoles into a dresser drawer.

"I don't know. I'm boiling in these dresses and stockings," said Falcon. "I wish Blinda would make us invisible so we could wear shorts."

Every day, while they cooked, or weeded, or walked, they told each other about their experiences with magic. Allie heard about Falcon's adventures with dragons and Falcon learned about life in the Ice Age. And in the evenings, after supper, they sat outside till it grew chilly and then went up to their quiet bedroom and talked long into the night.

*We make a good team,* thought Falcon as she and Allie stood in the kitchen of Blinda's house, putting together a particularly delicious lunch. The Montpellier butter stood ready in a yellow bowl. A side of salmon was poaching gently in white wine, and Allie was setting a platter of asparagus on the dining room table. Falcon had just taken a tray of buttery rolls out of the oven, and now she was hovering over a boiling pot of new potatoes.

After a few minor disasters, she had begun to get the knack

of having everything come out at the same time. She was learning to keep a sort of clock in her head so she'd know just when a sauce needed stirring or a chicken needed basting.

"It's like a dance," said Allie, covering the rolls with a linen napkin and putting them in the warming oven.

"What is?" asked Falcon. She tested a potato with the point of a knife and glanced at the simmering salmon.

"Cooking," Allie replied. "My mother says every activity has its own natural rhythm; you just have to find it." She watched as Falcon dumped the boiling potatoes into a colander in the sink, returned them to the pot, shook them over a low flame to dry them out, then added a lump of butter and a handful of minced parsley and set them on the back of the stove to stay hot.

"Like that," said Allie. "That was just beautiful." She carried the yellow bowl of Montpellier butter into the dining room and returned with a cut-glass pitcher. She filled it with lemonade from the big jar in the icebox, added some mint leaves from the garden, and cocked her head, listening.

"I hear Blinda and Emily. It would be nice if Mr. Quigley came today."

*If there's any salmon left,* thought Falcon, *I'll make a salad for lunch tomorrow, with cucumbers and watercress, and . . . No! I should be thinking about how to get back, not tomorrow's lunch.* She began cutting a lemon into wedges. Missy was always telling her, "You worry too much, little bird." Falcon crushed a mint leaf between her lemon-scented fingers and breathed in the fresh, sharp smell. *I'll worry later,* she decided.

"This is an extra *extra* yummy lunch," said Allie.

"It is, isn't it?" Falcon replied, and turned her attention to the salmon.

Blinda and Emily had walked across town and down to Charles Street. The witch marched a few steps ahead, her jaw set and an uncharacteristically grim look on her face. There had been arguments all morning: over a blue versus a brown frock, over oatmeal or sausages at breakfast, and over French lessons and a history test.

"I don't need all these tedious lessons," said Aunt Emily. "I'm already educated."

"We will stick to our normal schedule," said Blinda. "I don't want the servants getting any more suspicious. In any case, your French verbs are not at all what they should be."

When they finally did leave, Young Emily wanted to take a hansom cab and Aunt Emily wanted to go on the horsecars. In the end Blinda said, "We will walk, young lady, or ladies, and I have had just about enough!"

Emily walked a step or two behind the witch, and a good thing too, or Blinda would have seen her staggering from one side of the pavement to the other, muttering the whole time. Young Emily wanted to see one thing, Aunt Emily wanted to see another, and they could not—would not—agree. The truth is, the old Emily did not get along with her younger self at all, and vice versa. It isn't surprising, really, as there was a century of difference between them. The only thing they had in common was extreme stubbornness. Of course, as they were both stuck in the same body, this was a problem. By the time they got to Blinda's house, Emily was red-faced and furious.

Falcon carefully transferred the salmon to a big platter and garnished it with lemon wedges.

"There!" she said. She had been rather nervous about getting the salmon just right, but it was perfect. She liked what Allie had said about cooking and rhythm. Today it felt that way, the sound of simmering or the feel of a whisk beating the butter sauce to a velvety smoothness, the smell that told her the rolls were done, all of it coming together in a way that seemed almost magical.

*It is like a dance,* she thought. *And I think I might be good at it.* It was the first time she'd ever thought she could be good, *really* good, at anything. Her mother was an artist; her father was an ethnobotanist whose books on medicinal plants had made him almost famous. Great-Great-Aunt Emily had been a journalist and a fine pianist. *And if confidence counts, Toody will be anything he wants to be,* she thought. But she had never shown any particular talent, until now.

Thinking about Aunt Emily brought her back to reality. Here she was, stranded in 1903, her great-great-aunt stuck like a parasite in her younger self's head, and who knows whether they would ever get back to their own time? And if they did, what would happen to her aunt?

"What's wrong, Falcon?" asked Allie. She wiped the edges of the salmon platter with a damp towel and carried it into the dining room, where Humphrey Boggart was sitting at the table, knife and fork in hand, nose twitching at all the delicious smells coming out of the kitchen.

"Nothing," said Falcon. She tipped the parslied potatoes into a warm dish.

"There *is* something. You're worrying; I know you are," said Allie. "You always think Blinda is reading your mind, but anyone could do it—your face shows everything." She patted Falcon awkwardly on the shoulder. "It'll be okay, Falcon. I'm sure Blinda can help us. And this meal is . . ." Allie waved her hands, unable to put the perfection of Falcon's cooking into mere words.

Lunch was a great success. Blinda liked the Montpellier butter so much she said she wanted to put it on everything. The two Emilies hardly fought at all. Humphrey Boggart ate four helpings of everything and fell asleep in his chair, snoring loudly.

"He's getting a double chin," said Blinda, smiling down at the sleeping boggart. "Let's go out to the garden so we won't wake him." They tiptoed out of the cottage.

Blinda sat in one of the Adirondack chairs, and the three girls joined her around the table. The witch pulled several scraps of paper from a pocket in her skirt and smoothed them out, one by one.

"Have you found a way to get us home?" asked Falcon. "And Aunt Emily—what about making her well?" Blinda picked up the papers, fanning them out like a hand of cards.

"Spells," she said. "Involving spinning or leaping of one kind or another. Your brother was quite right, Allie. Time *is* like a series of carousels, and it's only a question of getting on the right one. Not difficult really. Any one of these will work.

And you, Allie, you're practically an expert. I daresay you three could do it without any help from me."

Falcon jumped up. "Well, let's go then, let's go now!"

"I'm sorry, Falcon. It's not as easy as that." Blinda put the spells back in her pocket.

"It's me, isn't it?" said Aunt Emily.

"I'm sorry," said the witch. "I can't fix that. I can't make you well, Emily, or young. Nobody can."

Falcon sank down in her chair.

"But then, if we go back . . ."

"I'll die," said Aunt Emily. Falcon turned to stare at her. Her great-great-aunt had never sounded so cold. The voice came out of a pink-cheeked twelve-year-old girl, but it made Falcon shiver. Emily stood up.

"I need a drink of water," she said and walked toward the house. The others sat in the garden without speaking. After a while Blinda suggested that they all have a cup of tea.

"It'll cheer us up and help us to think," she said. "There's nothing like a nice hot cup of—" The bright yellow door of the cottage crashed open and Humphrey Boggart staggered out. He had reverted to his natural shape, a pointy-eared little man. He was dressed in brown leather, and he wrung his hands and wept bright green tears.

"Ohhhh, I'm no good at all! A useless piece of nothing, I am, not fit to clean a troll's toenails! No, I'm not. Oh me, oh deary me!" He opened his mouth and wailed.

"Mercy, Humphrey, what on earth is it? It can't be all that bad. Calm down and tell us what's wrong." Blinda put an arm around the sobbing boggart and handed him a clean white handkerchief. He blew his nose, producing a remarkable quantity of snot, and drew a shuddering breath.

"She's gone!" he said. "You told me to watch them, the human girls, and I meant to, I really did, but I was so sleepy, and she said she only wanted a drink of water. How was I to know she'd sneak out the kitchen door?"

"Emily!" cried Blinda, Falcon, and Allie all together. They ran out to the sidewalk outside the stone wall. There was no sign of a girl in a blue dress and white pinafore, no sign at all.

# CHAPTER ELEVEN

THEY SEARCHED UP AND DOWN THE STREET AND looked in every room of Blinda's cottage, but Emily was nowhere to be found.

"Why would she go off like that?" asked Allie. Falcon grabbed Blinda's arm.

"She doesn't want to go back, does she? She doesn't want to go back because she knows she'll die. That's it, isn't it?" Blinda put her hand over Falcon's.

"I'm afraid so," she said.

"But you can help her, I know you can. We have to find her . . . Blinda! Maybe she's gone to see that magician, that Mr. Miracle. The one Mr. Quigley's always talking about."

The witch thought for a moment, rubbing her nose.

"It's quite possible. Maybe she thinks he can help her to stay in the past and never die."

"She wouldn't do that, she would never . . ." Falcon

stopped, remembering Aunt Emily's cold voice and the hard look on her face.

"Tony Pastor's is on 14th Street," said the witch. "Come on, we'll get a cab. It's not far."

"Oh, Blinda," said Falcon, "we don't have *time* for a cab. Can't you get us there more quickly?"

Blinda sighed. "People are in such a hurry these days," she said. "But no, you're quite right. We'd better find Emily as soon as possible, before she does anything foolish. Now, let's see . . ."

The witch led them back into the garden and had them all join hands and stand on tiptoe. She said, "East side, west side, all around the town. Take us to Tony Pastor's, it's the best show to be found."

For a moment nothing happened. Then, with a *whoosh* they were caught up in a great rush of wind that swept them from the cottage on Charles Street uptown to 14th Street and Broadway. They landed right in front of the theater entrance, much to Falcon's surprise. Most of the time Blinda's spells didn't work quite so efficiently. She turned to look at her companions and saw to her horror that it had *not* worked as well as she'd thought. Allie looked fine, if a little windblown, but the witch was half invisible.

"Oh drat," said Blinda. "I'm neither here nor there. Well, I'll likely solidify eventually. Come on, we've no time to waste." She hurried them into the theater, past a sign that read:

TONY PASTOR'S NEW FOURTEENTH STREET THEATER. CON-
TINUOUS PERFORMANCES FROM NOON TO MIDNIGHT DAILY.

REFINED ENTERTAINMENT FOR THE WHOLE FAMILY. FEA-
TURING THE AMAZING MR. MIRACLE, UNA MERKLE'S IM-
PERSONATIONS, THE REMARKABLE PROFESSOR SWIFT, AND
VERNON'S CORYBANTIC CANINES.

They were looking around the lobby at the bright posters on the walls, wondering how they would find Emily and Mr. Miracle, when a large woman in an usher's uniform approached them. She bumped into Blinda, and her eyes widened at the sight of the translucent witch.

"Oof!" said the woman. "Mind how you go, ma'am, didn't see you there." She peered at Allie and Falcon, and at the witch, who looked like a Blinda-shaped soap bubble. The usher fanned herself with the sheaf of programs she carried and wondered if she wasn't coming down with something. "Thin little thing, aren't you, ma'am? If you don't mind me sayin'. Here for the talent contest? You just go through that curtain at the back; there's a dressing room set aside for the amachoor acts. You're second on the bill, just after Mr. Gudgeon."

"Is he one of the actors? The man we're looking for is called Mr. Miracle," said Falcon.

"Oh, Gudgeon isn't so much a nactor, you know, as more of a song-and-dance man. The King of Unadilla, he calls his-self, and he's none too happy to be going first on the bill, nei-ther, poor feller. Mr. Pastor says if he don't get hisself a new act, he'll be out by summer. Now Mr. Miracle, he's something else. Second to last on the bill, played the Palace too. Amazing he is, just like the sign says. Though me, I like a nacrobat act, like them Flying DiMasseys." She led them to a hallway behind a

94

red plush curtain, handed them a program, and turned back to show people to their seats.

They huddled together in the dusty, dimly lit hall.

"We have to find Emily and get out of here," said Blinda. "Which do you suppose is Mr. Miracle's dressing room?"

They looked down the hallway, which was lined with doors. One of them, closest to the stage, had a star painted on it in gold.

"That must be it," said Falcon, pointing.

Just then, three people in glittering red, white, and blue costumes erupted out of the nearest door with a pack of assorted dogs, also in costume, scampering and leaping around them. None of them was barking except for a terrier in an orange ruff and plumed hat who gave an excited "YIP!" when he saw Allie and Falcon.

"Hush, Cappy!" said the older of the two women. "Down!"

"I told you he wasn't ready for the act," said the man, a tall, gloomy-looking person wearing a star-spangled top hat. "He'll ruin the hoop dance, you mark my words."

"He's fine, Vernon," said the woman, smiling at the three intruders. "Are you for the talent show? Your dressing room's just there." She pointed at a door on the left.

"Yes, thank you," said Blinda. "Oh, and by the way, could you tell us where Mr. Miracle might be? We admire him so." The woman smiled even more broadly, adjusting her scarlet sash.

"Just down the hall to the left, number three, with the star on the door. Now there's a class act, isn't he, Vernon? Though I believe he's off tonight. The Professor was going on in his place but he's . . . indisposed." She winked and mimed drinking.

"I'd be indisposed too if I had to be in with that Gudgeon. A real nervous Nelly, he is," said Vernon, straightening the tutu on a nearby poodle. He cocked his head, listening to the muffled roar of the crowd coming in and getting settled. "Come along, we've just got time to walk them before we're on!" The troupe moved swiftly down the hall toward a door that led into an alley as the band struck up "Under the Bim Bam Boo."

Blinda, Falcon, and Allie approached the door of Mr. Miracle's dressing room. Falcon tried to see through the keyhole, but something was hanging on the doorknob, blocking her view.

They heard footsteps approaching. Blinda hissed, "Quick! Here!" and flung open the door, shoving the girls in before her. They found themselves in a large room with a shelf running along one side. Several well-lighted mirrors hung over it, and in a chair, facing the mirror, sat a gray-haired man rubbing Albolene cream into his face to remove the greasepaint. He turned round as they burst in, and his eyebrows rose in astonishment at the sight of three strangers.

"'Pon my word!" he said. "Bit much this, really. Frightfully flattering and all that, but hardly the thing, you know! Who are you?" He was wearing the trousers of an evening suit over long johns; a towel was tucked in at his neck. Tubes of greasepaint and boxes of powder littered the shelf in front of him, and a golden halo the size of a dinner plate was propped against the mirror.

Falcon's face lit up.

"St. George!" she said. The saint (for indeed, it was he) looked embarrassed.

"Pardon me," he said. "'Fraid I haven't had the pleasure, young lady. Terrible with names, dontcha know. Saint . . . er, I mean, Mr. Miracle, at your service."

"Oh, but we're old friends," said Falcon. "Don't you remember, we . . ." Her voice trailed off as she realized that once again Time had turned everything upside down, and as far as St. George knew, they had never met.

By now the poor saint was quite bewildered.

"Oh dear," he said, "this is what comes of larking about on Earth; I should have known. They warned me, they did. And it was just this one last performance before the Gathering— that's all I wanted. Oh dear, oh dear." He extracted a large red bandanna from his trouser pocket and blew his nose with a sound like a trumpet. Falcon took pity on him and sat down beside him, putting a hand on his arm.

"It's all right, sir, really it is. If you'll just let me explain." She tried to make the story as simple as possible, but as St. George listened to her tale of time travel, Doublers, witches, and spells, his bushy eyebrows rose higher and higher on his forehead until she thought they would disappear into his hair. At last she paused for breath, and the saint wiped his brow with the bandanna.

"Good lord," he said, looking around at his visitors "A witch, you say. Met a lot of 'em, you know, alleged, in Heaven. Poor women, unjustly hanged or burned. Dreadful, really. People were so superstitious in my day. Now you say Miss Cholmondely is a real one? Beggin' your pardon, miss, but I'd no idea they were so, er . . . pretty." Blinda smiled at him, and he positively glowed.

"Can you help us?" asked Falcon. St. George sat twirling the halo between his hands for a moment, thinking.

"I haven't seen your aunt, m'dear. And whether I can help, well, sticky wicket, dontcha know, Time and all that. It'll have to wait until after the Gathering in any case. It's tonight, you see. And I am"—he shrugged modestly—"essential personnel, you might say. Otherwise, well, utter chaos, my dears, a perfect dog's dinner they'd make of it. I know! Why don't you come along and watch? Then afterward I'll see what I can do."

"And you're not going on here tonight, your, uh, holiness?" asked Allie.

"Oh no, not tonight. Did my farewell performance at the matinee. Must get back to Heaven, you see. Trying to get poor Mr. Gudgeon to take my spot, but Mr. Pastor just gave him a final warning. 'Get a new act,' says he, 'or you're out.'" St. George looked at the girls. "I don't suppose any of you can sing or dance, can you?" Falcon and Allie were shaking their heads when Emily charged into the room, dragging a fat little man by the hand.

"I can!" she said. "I know a lot of good songs too. I want to be in the amateur contest."

"Aunt Emily!" said Falcon. "Are you all right?"

"Of course I am! Why shouldn't I be? I came to see Mr. Miracle but look who I found. It's Mr. Gudgeon, my music teacher. *He's* the King of Unadilla!" The little man wore an ill-fitting suit of black tie and tails and a stunned expression, like someone who has just lived through a tornado.

"I knew I'd heard that name somewhere," said Blinda. She

held out her hand. "Mr. Gudgeon, how delightful to meet you at last. But, Emily, it's quite impossible. Your parents would never allow you to go on the stage." Falcon thought she sounded like someone reciting a rule she didn't actually believe in.

"My parents," retorted Young Emily, "are not here."

"And," said Aunt Emily, "if I have to go back, at least I should get a chance to go onstage first. It's one of the few things I've always regretted not doing."

Blinda sighed. "Oh, all right. But just this once. It's such a novelty to hear you two agreeing for a change."

"No, no, no," said St. George. "Not the amateur contest. I've a much better idea—simply spiffing. You go on with Gudgeon here—help him out. What d'ye say, young-feller-me-lad? You've just time to rehearse a bit before you go on." Pink with excitement, the saint led Emily and the bewildered Gudgeon out the door.

Before the others had time to catch their breath, the dressing room was invaded by a stout woman carrying a viola and dragging a small boy with long blond ringlets.

"Hello," said Blinda. "Are you here for the contest? This is Mr. Miracle's dressing room. The amateurs are down the hall." The woman drew herself up and peered down at Blinda and the others from behind her formidable violet silk bosom.

"We do *not* consider ourselves amateurs. I am Mrs. Amaryllis Fotherington-Hay and this is Parsifal Fotherington-Hay, the International Child Prodigy." It was hard not to stare at the little boy. He was dressed in a black velvet suit with knee pants and a big lace collar, and he wore a wide-brimmed plumed hat over his yellow curls. He had a round, goggle-eyed face and an expression of self-satisfied stupidity that reminded Falcon of a toad.

Allie smiled at him and held out her hand. "How are you, Parsifal? Are you going to sing a song in the contest?"

Parsifal Fotherington-Hay looked at Allie's outstretched hand as though it might explode.

"I don't shake hands with strangers," he said.

"Microbes," said Mrs. Fotherington-Hay. "Parsifal does not sing. He recites selections from the Great Poets while I accompany him on the violin-cello." She took the little boy's hand. "Come, precious, it's time for your hot lemon and honey."

"Aw, Ma," said Parsifal. "I hate that stuff! Can't I have a Moxie instead?"

Mrs. Fotherington-Hay's face stiffened.

"Now, precious, Mummy knows best, and you know Mummy likes you to call her 'Dearest.'" As they left the room, a man carrying a clipboard stuck his head in the door. He consulted the list in his hand and frowned. "This ain't liberty hall, ya know. Who are youse? I don't see you on my list for the amachoor contest."

"We're with Mr. Miracle," said Blinda, smiling. "Family." The man's stern face relaxed into a friendly grin.

"Oh! Beg pardon, miss. Mr. Miracle's fambly's always welcome here. You go on out front and I'll see Miss O'Malley gives you the best seats fer the show. Now where are them sand dancers?" He made a check mark on his list with a pencil stub and shut the door.

Falcon, Allie, and Blinda made their way to the theater lobby, where they were again greeted by the usher. She gave them a broad smile, which broadened even more when she saw Blinda. The witch had become almost solid by now.

"Katy O'Malley at yer service, ladies, and Mr. Perkins says I'm to give you the best seats in the house. Follow me." They made their way into the gilded, red plush music hall, where Miss O'Malley showed them to three comfortable chairs on the aisle.

People were coming in, making quite a racket, while two jugglers tossed balls and clubs in the air to the sound of the band playing Sousa marches. Allie felt sorry for the jugglers; nobody was paying any attention to them at all.

"They must have moved the King of Unadilla to a better spot on the bill," said Blinda. Sure enough, the jugglers ran off-stage as the lights went down, and an elegantly dressed man with a big mustache strutted onto the stage.

"I do believe that's Tony Pastor himself," said Blinda. Mr. Pastor waited till the audience was quiet and motioned to the bandleader. The band began playing a familiar tune very softly as Mr. Pastor said, "Ladeeze and Gennelmun, fresh from the stages of Yurrup and Paree, that salubrious sultan of southern song, the King of Unadilla and his darling Dixie queen!"

Falcon held her breath as the music grew louder. *What if Aunt Emily is terrible? What if she makes a complete fool of herself in front of all these people? What if . . .*

She gasped as Mr. Gudgeon and Emily ran onto the stage. Emily wore a fluffy pink dress, white stockings and shoes, and a huge pink bow in her hair. Mr. Gudgeon, still in his baggy suit, was transformed. His face shone with confidence as he and Emily launched into the song Falcon had heard a hundred times.

Come on, everybody, come on by,
Come onna my house for mammy's pie.
Apple or lemon, dontcha be shy,
Come have a piece of huckleberry pie!

H-U-uckle-uckle, B-U-buckle-buckle,
That spells huckleberry pie!
H-U-uckle-uckle, B-U-buckle-buckle,
That spells huckleberry pie!

The audience chuckled. While Emily sang the next verse, the King of Unadilla broke into a shuffling, loose-jointed dance that made everyone laugh and applaud. Emily's voice soared above the noise.

If your little baby's got a tear in his eye,
Fetch him a piece of mammy's pie.
Mincemeat, Nesselrode, ya just gotta try
My old mammy's huckleberry pie!

Mr. Gudgeon joined her on the chorus, and she joined him in doing a very competent soft-shoe.

"I didn't know your aunt could dance," Allie said. Falcon looked on in amazement.

"Neither did I. They're really good!" Gudgeon began a shoulder-shrugging, sliding step and Emily stepped to one side. The crowd roared, and someone in the cheap seats yelled, "Snake hips! Go 'er, Chollie!" Emily began the last verse:

Only one thing'll make a strong man cry,
And that is a piece of mammy's pie.
You'll feel better, by and by,
Come on over for some huckleberry pie!

Everybody joined in on the final chorus, and when it was over there was pandemonium. People cheered and shouted, "Encore! Encore!"

Gudgeon signaled the band to play another chorus, and the crowd sang along as before.

Blinda nudged Falcon and Allie, who were singing happily. "Come on, let's meet them backstage, away from this mob." They made their way back to St. George's dressing room to wait. The saint, who had watched the whole performance from the wings, was puffed up with pride.

"I say!" he said. "Jolly fine show, what? Absolutely tickety-boo, if I do say it myself!" He clapped Emily on the back as she charged through the door, cheeks as pink as her dress. Falcon and Allie chattered with excitement, and even Blinda gave her approval.

"You did extremely well, Emily. Perhaps, as your parents already know Mr. Gudgeon, they might permit you to continue, as long as you keep up with your schoolwork. And we won't tell them anything just yet, in any case." Emily threw her arms around the witch.

"I *was* good, wasn't I?" said Young Emily. "And Mr. Gudgeon was wonderful! He said that kind of dancing is called 'eccentric dancing,' and he never thought it went with the song he was singing."

"But I taught him the huckleberry pie song and I'm going to teach him more, like 'Everybody Works but Father' and 'Don't Dilly Dally with Sally,'" said Aunt Emily.

"But, Emily, perhaps those songs haven't been written yet," said Blinda.

"Well, they ought to be." Falcon knew it was her aunt speaking, but the stubborn look could have belonged to either of the Emilies. *Maybe people don't change all that much when they grow up,* she thought.

Blinda's mouth tightened, and St. George began twiddling a silver dollar through his fingers in an amazingly dexterous way. It was a magician's habit he had picked up, and it soothed him when he was nervous.

"Not a good idea, you know, muddling with Time like that. Songs yet unwritten . . . dangerous, very. Unforeseen consequences."

"But Mr. Gudgeon is talking to Tony Pastor right now. He wants to put us on in Mr. Miracle's place. He *loved* us!"

"I'll talk to him," said Blinda. "We'll see about you, Emily, continuing with this after . . ." She peered into Young Emily's flushed face. "After *you,* Emily, have gone back to your own time."

"Yes!" said Young Emily. "You have to go. This is *my* life, not yours. They're sending me to boarding school next year and I'll never have another chance like this. Ow! Stop that!" She grimaced and put her hands to the sides of her head.

"Enough!" said Blinda in a voice that startled them with its harshness. The witch stalked out of the dressing room, leaving all of them silent and Emily as white as she had been pink before. St. George spun the dollar so quickly through his fingers that it became a gleaming blur.

"Oh dear, oh dear," he said. "Not the thing at all, is it? Oh dear."

"I don't care," said Aunt Emily. "It's not fair! I want to stay here." Blinda came back.

"Mr. Gudgeon will take St. George's place on his own tonight. It was the new song and his dancing that Mr. Pastor particularly liked. As for you, Emily, we'll see." She held up a hand as Emily (*both of them,* thought Falcon) started to protest.

"*I said, we'll see!* Now then, your blessedness, may we join you for the Gathering?"

Blinda's words galvanized St. George. He leapt up and clapped on his halo.

"The Gathering! 'Pon my word, I nearly forgot. Must hurry, no time to waste, long way to go, you see." They followed him out of the theater by a back door.

# CHAPTER TWELVE

I T WAS EARLY EVENING BY THE TIME THEY EMERGED
from Tony Pastor's, and for a moment they were disoriented by the darkening sky and the bright lights of 14th Street. But St. George knew his way around the theater district. He led them at a fast trot toward Union Square.

"Where are we going?" asked Allie.

"To Central Park," said Aunt Emily, her eyes sparkling. "It's April 23rd, isn't it, Blinda, even though we left on the 22nd and have been here more than a week."

"Yes," answered the witch. "St. George's Day. The Gathering."

"I don't care where you go, but you have to get out of my body," said Young Emily.

"Not before the . . . not tonight, I won't. Just try and make me!" Aunt Emily retorted. The witch shot her a warning glance as St. George tried to wave down a hansom cab. But Union

Square was bustling with traffic, and all the cabs seemed to be occupied. They rumbled right past without stopping.

"Oh, I say, it's after eight o'clock. We'll never get there on time," said the saint.

Blinda rummaged in her pockets.

"Aha!" she said, waving a scrap of paper. "My latest spell. It's just the thing." She stretched her arms out straight. "Give me room," she said. They backed off, and St. George, who found magic rather nerve-racking, crossed his fingers.

Blinda began to bounce up and down, reciting the new spell: "Oughta be faster. Oughta be swift. Give me a ride. And give me a lift. Speed like lightning, sleek as an eel. Oughta be here NOW! Auto-mo-bile!"

Nothing happened. Everybody looked embarrassed. St. George said, "Never mind, Miss Cholmondely, I'll just get us a cab and—"

KABOOM!

The explosion rattled the windows of every building round Union Square and surrounded the witch with a cloud of purple smoke that smelled of lilacs and gasoline. They heard her coughing and saying, "Oh drat, drat, and double drat!"

The cloud dissipated to reveal Blinda, with a lavender smudge on her cheek, sitting in a most remarkable vehicle.

It was painted bright red and most of it seemed to be made of metal. It had no roof, and the seats were made of green, scaly leather. The back tapered into a long, sleek tail tipped with an arrowhead point, but it was the front of the machine that was most astonishing. It stretched out into the largest hood ornament ever: a dragon's head with gold-rimmed scales and a crest that would surely block the driver's view of the road. The saint stepped forward to touch the car's gleaming surface.

"No finger smudges, *if* you please," said a voice. The dragon opened its eyes and snorted a warning blast of steam. St. George jumped.

"Oh!" he said. "Beg pardon. Didn't know you were alive, old thing."

"You don't know much, by the look of you," said the car.

"It's a dragonmobile!" said Emily.

"Yes, drat it . . . It's not quite right. I can't do spells properly when I'm not entirely visible," said Blinda.

"Not right?" said the car. "I am the most perfect thing you will ever see, unlike some insubstantial people I could mention."

"Get in," said Blinda. "We've got to hurry." The others climbed into the dragonmobile; Emily and Blinda sat in front, Allie and Falcon in back, and the saint in the rumble seat. They could feel the warm vibration of the dragon-powered engine under their bottoms. Blinda put the car in drive and they took off with a bang and a puff of purple exhaust. St. George shut his eyes as they soared into the sky over Union Square.

They went zooming through the air thirty feet above Broadway, heading uptown so fast that, unless they looked straight ahead, all they could see was a blur.

"M-M-M-Miss Cholmondely, don't you think you ought to slow down?" said St. George, who was holding on for dear life.

"No time to waste, your saintliness!" said Blinda, narrowly missing the top of a tree. St. George closed his eyes and wished he had not eaten so many crullers for tea. The car was flying over Central Park, looking for a place to land.

Allie's nose twitched like a rabbit's.

"What's that smell?" she said. "Is something burning?" Indeed there was a smoky haze in the air, visible in the light of the streetlamps that stood at intervals along the paths. They did little to illuminate the darkness, and the deep shadows under the trees looked capable of hiding any number of mysteries.

They descended rapidly and came to a sudden stop at Belvedere Castle, just south of the Great Lawn. Fortunately, nobody was hurt and, rather shakily, they climbed out of the car.

"Sorry," said Blinda. "I haven't quite got the hang of driving yet."

"Not bad for a beginner," said the car.

There were only a few people walking on the paths, on their way out of the park now that night was falling. The odd thing was that nobody seemed to notice either them or the unusual car.

"It's just temporary," said Blinda. "I didn't have time to do a full invisibility spell, but it will do." Sure enough, no one gave them a second or even a first glance as they walked up the path with the dragonmobile trundling along behind them, eyeing the people strolling on the path in a rather greedy manner.

"Something *is* burning," said Allie, peering through the gloom.

They were approaching the intersection of several paths near the Great Lawn. The dragonmobile began to pant, sending short puffs of purple steam into the air.

"Mercy mercy Maud," it gasped. "I never thought I'd see

it—no, I never. Mumsy would be so proud. Oh mercy!" It gave a loud *CLANK* and all four tires suddenly went flat with a *whoosh*.

"He's fainted," said Blinda. The others never even noticed. They were riveted by what was happening on the Great Lawn.

The dragons were coming.

One by one they flew through the darkness from places seldom seen by human eyes. From the bleak deserts of North Africa, where the nomads took them for sandstorms, they came. From the deep Amazonian jungle and the endless forests of Russia, they came. From the Canadian woodlands, where hunters tell dragon tales through the long winter nights, they came. From the trackless white expanses of the poles and the barren reaches of the Mongolian steppes; from the heights of Annapurna; from the vast and heaving sea—more amazing, more terrible than waterspouts or giant squid or great white sharks—they came! Large and small, a year out of the egg or as old as Time: red dragons from Wales and Ireland and Cornwall; green dragons from Tibet; long golden dragons from China; silvery web-footed dragons from all the oceans; and those rare blue dragons from the North Pole who live on icebergs and blast fishing holes through the frozen sea for their friends the polar bears. The smoky haze came from their taloned feet as they touched down, scorching the new spring grass of the Great Lawn, and the stars of the April night were dimmed by the glow of their flaming wings.

The three girls walked to the edge of the lawn, where they stood, enchanted.

"No closer; you'll be burnt to a crisp," Blinda warned

them. She had seen the Gathering of the Dragons almost every year since she was a little girl in 1700, and though she still found it exciting and beautiful, it was hardly awe-inspiring. She glanced at the three, all beglamored on the edge of the lawn, and snorted.

"Humans," she said. "So easily distracted." St. George straightened his halo.

"Thanks awfully, Miss Cholmondely. Extraordinary, er . . . ride, really. Now if you'll excuse me. Got to change into armor and all that—you know, saint gear. Have to get these dragons warmed up, so to speak. *Haw haw.*" He waited for a laugh that didn't come. "Warmed up, you see. Bit of a pun. Dragons are already hot, dontcha know." He sighed and walked off into the bushes.

The three girls and the witch stood close together, watching the dragons. Then, from the far end of the Great Lawn, a low, insistent tune began to wind through the spring night. Faint at first—here a flute, there an oboe, now a drum—the notes rose into the sky like smoke until the air was filled with music. Emily, Falcon, and Allie listened in amazement, for there were no musicians to be seen.

St. George emerged from the bushes dressed in a shining suit of chain mail, his halo set rakishly on the back of his head. He twirled his mustache and sauntered toward the horde of dragons; their fiery bodies made the air shimmer with heat. All of them stood poised to begin the dance. The dark sky grew brighter and brighter, and the people watching had to shade their eyes against the brilliant glow as the music soared. And then, descending on a shaft of moonlight came the greatest dragon of all, the Seeing One, source of all Magic. Blue lightning flickered around her head as she landed in a swirl of flame and arched her wings to begin the dance. The music filled the night as St. George raised his hands and the Gathering of the Dragons began. The four friends climbed the big boulder at the edge of Turtle Pond to watch as St. George led the dragon dancers late into the night, till the sky turned from black to dark blue and the shadows began to lighten.

Then, one by one, the dragons flew away until only the Seeing One remained and the music stopped. St. George turned toward the great dragon as she bent her long neck down to hear him speak. After a moment she raised her head, casting her sapphire gaze on the girls with such tenderness that tears came to their eyes, though they could not have said why. Then the Seeing One spread her wings and rose into the sky through a tornado of fire that whirled around the saint as he raised his arm in farewell.

"Won't she burn him?" asked Falcon anxiously, watching the flames leap around him, turning his silvery armor to gold.

"Of course not," said Blinda, getting up and rolling her shoulders to get the kinks out. "He's a saint—it'll just give him a nice rosy glow. He can join us when he's cooled off. Now then, let's go home and have some breakfast."

# CHAPTER THIRTEEN

THE DRAGONMOBILE COMPLAINED ALL THE WAY home.

"My one chance to see the Gathering and you just let me lie there—you didn't wake me up. Thoughtless I call it, just like a witch."

"You *did* faint," said Falcon.

"Oh, of course, take her side! You would, you . . . human! But it's only me, isn't it, a mere machine, no feelings, oh no . . . just scales and tin . . ." At last the car, with smoky puffs of self-pity, landed them in front of Blinda's cottage on Charles Street.

They had their breakfast just after dawn, sitting in the garden. Humphrey Boggart dragged a small armchair out of the living room for St. George, who arrived—still glowing—just as the food was served. When he sat down, the upholstery smoldered slightly and Blinda made a mental note to re-cover the chair. The boggart had taken a great liking to Allie and kept plying her with homemade boggart goodies: green snot marmalade, toad vomit cream, hot dandruff biscuits. Allie, who had grown very fond of Humphrey, had great difficulty refusing until Falcon explained that they were all on a strict regimen of "people food" only. At this the boggart showed great sympathy and retired to the kitchen to wrap up a jar of cat-poop pickle for them to enjoy when they were off their diets.

Blinda supplied them with a delicious people-food breakfast, all of which she pulled out of the air without any mistakes at all. Well, it is true that the first round of sausages arrived crisp, brown, and *alive,* wriggling off the plate and scampering into the bushes with loud squeals of indignation. But the second batch was everything that sausages should be, and everyone enjoyed them very much, especially the saint, who loved earthly food. Emily, however, ate almost nothing. She broke a piece of toast into smaller and smaller pieces and hardly spoke until they were finished eating and had gone on to tea and coffee.

"Are you quite well, Miss Emily?" asked St. George, mopping at a blob of jam on his armor. Emily tried to smile at him, but it was a sad, sorry excuse for a smile.

"Thank you, St. George. I'm just not very hungry," said Young Emily.

"Neither am I," said Aunt Emily. "And, Blinda, you know quite well why."

She turned to the saint, who was trying to decide whether eating a fourth popover would be sinfully gluttonous. "Can you help me, sir?" St. George dropped the jam spoon.

"Oh, blast," he said. He looked at Emily sadly.

"Oh, my dear, I asked her, you know, the Seeing One. If anyone could help, she could. She is outside Time. But the other

thing . . . well. How do you feel, if you don't mind my asking?"
Emily rubbed her temples.

"I have a terrible headache," said Young Emily.

"The headache is me, isn't it?" Aunt Emily sounded flat
and dull.

Blinda drank the last of her tea and set the cup down in its
saucer. She took Emily's hand.

"Emily, I'm sorry. I can't help you. No magic can help you,
not in the way you want. You can't stay in Young Emily's body,
and you have to go back."

"To die," said Aunt Emily. She turned to the saint, but he
only nodded once and looked away. "I hate it!" she said. "I
don't want to die—why should I? I could stay here forever and
never grow old."

"No you can't!" said Young Emily. "I don't want you in
here. There's no room—I can't breathe!" Her hands began to
claw frantically at her own throat as she turned her head this
way and that to escape her own fingernails. Nearly in tears,
Falcon seized her hands and held them tight.

"Oh, don't, please don't! Blinda, can't you do *something?*"

"I can't," said the witch. "I'm sorry, but I can't. No one can."

"It's not that I'm afraid!" Aunt Emily cried. "I just don't
want to die. What's wrong with that?" Nobody knew what to
say. At last Blinda spoke.

"Oh, my dear, don't you see? If you stay here in the body
of your young self, you will never grow up. Your old self will
gradually take over Young Emily's mind because you are
stronger than she, and because . . . because your desire, your
rage to live, is so fierce. If you do this, then all the experiences

she should have had, all the feelings she would have felt, will never happen. She will never fall in love, never know grief or joy or passion, never work and learn and grow as you have. She will never have the chance to be the person you have become. And after a long time, you will begin to fade too, until there is only a twelve-year-old *thing* named Emily, living forever but never growing up. Such a being is called a Time Wraith, and it is a most terrible thing to be." Blinda paused. "And Emily, if you stay here, you will never know Falcon." The witch's words fell into silence. Everyone watched Emily, who sat a little apart from them, her lips pressed together and her eyes shining with unshed tears. *She looks so alone,* thought Falcon. *I can't bear it.*

"It's not fair!" Falcon said, clenching her fists. "You can't die, you just can't! Blinda, St. George, you have to help." Aunt Emily smiled shakily.

"You look just as you did when I first met you, Falcon, on the day you were born. Red-faced and hitting out with both fists. Emily is right. I don't fit in her head; I don't fit in this time. It's just the way things are."

She reached out to her niece, and at her touch Falcon's anger crumbled and she sank to the ground, sobbing. Emily held her until she was calm, her cheek against Falcon's hair.

Falcon sniffled. St. George handed her his napkin, and she wiped her eyes and blew her nose. Emily's face seemed to blur so that Falcon could see both Young Emily and Aunt Emily beneath the skin. She spoke in a voice so low they had to lean forward to hear her.

"I love my life," Aunt Emily said. "I love watching the dawn from my bedroom each day, and the taste of morning tea. I love walking in the park on the first autumn day and watching the chandelier rise into the ceiling at Lincoln Center before the overture begins. I've seen the Gathering of the Dragons, and now I've seen it twice!" She paused to look at her niece, and her voice grew husky.

"But most of all, Falcon, I love you, and I had hoped to see you grow into the fine woman you will become. I hate it that I won't. I *hate* it." She took a deep breath and sat looking down at her hands for a long time. At last she stood up, smoothed her hair, and cleared her throat.

"Blinda, can you get us back without turning us into bandicoots?" The witch shook her head.

"You don't need me for this. You can do it yourself, the three of you. You're all Magnets. You just have to spin." Emily, Falcon, and Allie hugged Blinda, St. George, and even Humphrey. The boggart was deeply affected by this and turned into a wombat out of sheer sentiment. The three girls moved to the center of the garden.

"Goodbye, your saintliness," said Falcon, looking at him where he stood beside Blinda, trying not to cry. "I'll see you in . . . I *will* have seen . . . I mean . . . oh, goodbye, goodbye!"

"Goodbye," said Allie, hoping the witch was right about time travel and that they wouldn't end up in the Ice Age or worse. The three girls took each other's hands and began to turn in a circle. The garden seemed to blur as they spun faster. A fog of pink and blue and yellow rose out of Emily's head, and the last thing they saw was Young Emily standing on the lawn next to Blinda, waving and calling, "Goodbye, goodbye!"

# CHAPTER FOURTEEN

T HEY SPUN AND SWIRLED THROUGH COOL GRAY
mist until, after a time, the mist began to clear and
they landed without the slightest bump on Great-Great-Aunt
Emily's Persian rug in the living room on East 66th Street. Allie wondered whether they were getting better at time travel
or whether the magic was being considerate on account of
Aunt Emily's age.

There they were, the three of them, Falcon and Allie kneel-
ing on the rug with Emily between them. Falcon had grown so
used to seeing her aunt in Young Emily's body that it was a
shock to see her so old again. She had always taken her aunt's
age for granted. Now she seemed to see it for the first time. She
cradled Emily, feeling the old woman's face, soft and cool
against her arm. Her aunt's skin was thin and translucent, so
the blue veins showed through, and it had a crumpled texture
like dried rose petals. The bones of her face were clearly out-

lined beneath. Falcon remembered all the stories Emily had told her. *Her whole life is in her skin,* she thought, *in her bones and in her walk. She is her own history.* All those years of sun and wind, water from all the rivers and oceans of the world, insect bites from a hundred jungles. Moles and spots and blotches. A fine white line through one eyebrow, cut by flying glass during an air raid in France. A slight limp from a riding accident in Scotland; a bump from a badly set collarbone broken on a visit to Pancho Villa's hideout in the mountains of Mexico; a scar like a seam on her left forearm from a fall on Mt. Kilimanjaro, the fractured elbow held out from her body ever after, like a broken wing. Her white hair was still abundant but it had no shine. Her eyes that had once been the color of a winter sea had faded to palest gray. Her teeth were yellowed by more than a hundred years of tea and coffee, their edges worn by a century of chewing through thousands of meals. Her voice, when she spoke, was so faint that Falcon had to bend down to hear her.

"I've loved it. I've loved it *all,*" she whispered.

"Aunt Emily, I . . ." Falcon's arms tightened around her aunt as though she could keep death away with her own young strength. Her eyes blurred, and a tear fell onto Emily's up-turned face.

"I don't want you to go! Please don't, please!" she begged With one last effort, Great-Great-Aunt Emily reached up to Falcon's cheek, her touch light as a moth's wing. The old woman's face was full of light.

"My dearest girl," she said. And died.

★　　★　　★

Falcon was never sure how long they sat there in the still, silent room while the dusk gathered outside the windows.

"How beautiful she is," said Allie. She heard the note of surprise in her own voice. "I never saw it."

"She always was," said Falcon, understanding it for the first time. *It's who she was,* she thought. *Not her face or her body or her age.* "She looked like . . . herself," she said.

"You are so much like her," said Allie, "and so much like yourself. My friend in the Ice Age, he was that way too. At first I thought he was hideous, but then I saw how beautiful he was."

After a while Allie went to the phone and called Missy because Falcon did not want to leave Emily.

"Your father is there; they're both coming." Allie sat down beside Falcon and clasped her arms around her knees.

"Sometimes I think I see my friend's face, or part of his face, in a crowd," she said. "Once there was a guy in front of me in swim class who looked just like him from the back. I almost thought it *was* him, till he turned around."

"Oh, do you swim?" said Falcon absently, looking down at Emily's peaceful face. "So do I. The Sportsplex."

"That's where I go," said Allie. "Maybe we could go together sometime. I'm Intermediate."

Falcon told Allie about her disintegrating bathing suit. "Your mother helped me. She was really kind."

"You must have just *died,*" said Allie, suddenly gasping with horror at her own words.

"Omigosh, I didn't mean . . . I'm sorry!" Falcon reached out and took Allie's hand.

"I know you didn't. It's okay, Allie, it really is. I just wish I'd told Aunt Emily. It would've made her laugh."

The door opened and Missy and Peter rushed in. There was a confusion of tears and hugs, and Allie stood uncomfortably by, not knowing what to do.

"I should go," she said.

"Oh no," said Falcon, turning in Missy's embrace. "You've been part of this from the beginning, and you're a Magnet too. It makes us like sisters." Missy put her arms around them both.

"So. She told you before she died. And you too, Allie. How extraordinary. I'll take you home in a cab, dear, shall I, and then come back?" Allie couldn't speak. She had begun to cry without making a sound. Tears ran down her face as she hugged Falcon goodbye and walked out into the hallway, toward the elevator, with Missy's arm around her. Peter made some phone calls and then joined Falcon on the rug beside Emily.

"So, my bird, now *you* are the one, the Magic Magnet in our family, as Emily has been for more than a hundred years. I feel in awe of you. I don't know what to say." He rubbed a hand over his eyes.

"Oh, don't!" said Falcon. "Don't be in awe—it makes me feel so lonely. I feel so empty with Emily gone. Don't be in awe, please!"

"You still have Emily. You always will, in your mind and heart, as long as you remember her. So will I," said Peter.

"But I hate that she's dead! I want her to be *really* here, with cups of tea and teasing and telling stories."

"And arguing. Don't forget arguing," said her father, his voice breaking.

They sat for a long time with their arms around each other as the moon rose and the stars came out and the sounds of the city changed from day to night. And somewhere, in a place outside of here or there or when, where dragons danced and dreamers dreamed, a girl named Emily was laughing.